Could it last forever?

Removing the necklace my mother had given me earlier in the evening, Parker fastened the clasp of the Tiffany one around my neck. "Now, that does you justice," he said, bending forward to kiss me. "You're so beautiful. I love you, Rose."

It was the first time he'd said that. My eyes widened in surprise, but I closed them as our lips touched. Parker Kemp loved me!

Our kiss went on and on. Parker's friends clapped and whistled, but we still didn't draw apart.

Fifteen had been a terrible year—I'd lost my father. The year I turned sixteen was bound to be better. One thing's for sure, I thought, dizzy with happiness. It's off to a great start.

Don't miss any books in this dramatic new series:

THE YEAR

I TURNED

Sixteen

#1 Rose
#2 Daisy
#3 Laurel
#4 Lily

Available from ARCHWAY Paperbacks

THE YEAR
I TURNED
Sixteen

ROSE

Diane Schwemm

AN ARCHWAY PAPERBACK
Published by POCKET BOOKS
New York London Toronto Sydney Tokyo Singapore

This book is a work of fiction. Names, characters, places, and
incidents are either products of the author's imagination or
are used fictitiously. Any resemblance to actual events or locales
or persons, living or dead, is entirely coincidental.

AN ARCHWAY PAPERBACK *Original*

An Archway Paperback published by
POCKET BOOKS, a division of Simon & Schuster Inc.
1230 Avenue of the Americas, New York, NY 10020

Produced by Seventeenth Street Productions, Inc., New York

Copyright © 1998 by Daniel Weiss Associates, Inc., and
Diane Schwemm
Cover art copyright © 1998 by Daniel Weiss Associates, Inc.

ISBN: 0-671-00440-9

First Archway Paperback printing July 1998

10 9 8 7 6 5 4 3 2

AN ARCHWAY PAPERBACK and colophon are
registered trademarks of Simon & Schuster Inc.

Printed in the U.S.A.

IL 7+

For Heather and Laura,
my sisters and best friends.

One

Sometimes I wish I didn't live in a small town.

Hawk Harbor is the kind of place where everybody knows everybody else. There's one grocery store and one gas station and one bank. We have to share a high school with a bunch of other towns. We don't even have our own exit off the Maine Turnpike.

And needless to say, the nightlife is rather limited.

Now and then I find myself wondering what it would be like to live someplace crowded and exciting. Those are the days I can't wait to graduate and move to New York or L.A.

Then there are days like today, May 21, my sixteenth birthday, when I can't imagine living anywhere else. This afternoon on my way in from school I stopped on the porch of my family's Victorian house. Standing on tiptoe, I could see a distant sliver of the Atlantic, past the pines and the rocky shore. The water was speckled with sailboats and fishing trawlers that reminded me of my dad's old boat, the *Pelican*.

Summer is just around the corner, and that means pretty soon I'll be heading off to be a counselor at Wildwood, a camp in Vermont. I can't wait.

I want to be a singer, and Wildwood is a performance camp—I won a scholarship there a few years ago, and I've been going every summer. There aren't many opportunities to get musical training in rural Maine, so Wildwood was a total stroke of luck. Plus it's my only opportunity all year to get a taste of independence.

Inside the house I could tell right away that my mother, Maggie Walker, had been chopping and roasting and sifting and baking all afternoon. She's an awesome cook and always goes all out for special occasions, but this morning I'd told her it was fine if we skipped the festivities. After all, no one's been in the mood for a party for three months. Why would anything be different today? But she just hugged me and said, "My oldest girl is turning sixteen. That only happens once in a lifetime."

Seeing the tears in her blue eyes, I felt I couldn't argue with that.

I dumped my book bag on the living room couch and followed my nose to the kitchen. "Happy birthday, Rose," my thirteen-year-old sister Daisy called out from the dining room.

"Happy birthday!" echoed ten-year-old Laurel and eight-year-old Lily.

"Hi, everybody," I responded. "Smells great, Mom!" I walked into the dining room and watched Daisy set the table with the good china, carefully placing every napkin and utensil just so. Her long blond ponytail was pulled through the back of her Boston Red Sox cap, which I suspect she sleeps in.

(I know for a fact that until she was eleven she slept with her autographed Carl Yastrzemski baseball mitt under her pillow.) I couldn't help noticing that in spite of her usual uniform of gym shorts and T-shirt, she's starting to get really pretty. Of course, she'd probably punch me if I said so. When the guys on her baseball team started telling her that last year, she switched to all-girls' softball.

I opened my mouth to tell Daisy how nice the table looked but was interrupted. "It's my turn to lick the beaters," Lily whined from the kitchen.

"Uh-oh," I said, and Daisy rolled her eyes in a here-we-go-again look.

We both peeked through the doorway into the kitchen, anticipating a good show. Sure enough, Mom had just made the chocolate frosting for my birthday cake and Laurel had, naturally, seized the beaters. She's going through a growth spurt or something and consumes about half her weight in food a day. She's currently about a foot taller than Lily. So there was Laurel, holding one beater high above Lily's head and licking the other while Lily danced up and down, fuming.

I couldn't help laughing. Lily likes to dress up, and the costume du jour consisted of the calico skirt I had worn in our high school production of *Oklahoma!* last year, a hot pink tube top that wasn't staying up very well, and clip-on pearl earrings. For some reason her blond pigtails were sticking straight out from the sides of her head. Laurel was a sight, too: cutoff jeans, scraped knees, and a grass-stained shirt. "Personally,

I wouldn't want to eat anything she just touched, but that's me," I said to Daisy under my breath.

Laurel turned bright red. She doesn't like to fight, but she has a real stubborn streak—especially when she knows she's right. "It's not your turn," she informed Lily. "You got the beaters when Mom made carrot cake for the church potluck two weeks ago."

"No, I didn't!" screeched Lily—who does like to fight—as she stamped her small feet.

"Time-out," called Daisy. "Hand one over, Laurel."

"Why should I?" asked Laurel. "Possession is nine-tenths of the law, and Lily doesn't have the right to—ow!"

Laurel's speech was interrupted by the kick in the shin Lily gave her. With a yelp Laurel dropped both beaters on the kitchen floor and started hopping around in pain.

"Okay, that's enough," Mom declared, scooping up the beaters and dumping them into the soapy water in the sink. "If you can't agree, then nobody gets any beaters. Now, take it outside, you two. And don't come back in until you've made up."

Lily and Laurel disappeared, but I could still hear them bickering as I headed upstairs to my room. Oh, well, what can you do? *Sisters*.

Since I was going out later, I put on the blue sleeveless dress I'd just bought on sale at Harrington's Department Store. It had taken all the birthday money my grandparents in Florida had sent me, but it was worth it.

As my family gathered for dinner I noticed that my sisters looked relatively presentable, too. Of course Mom looked beautiful—she always does. She'd tossed aside her apron and brushed out her shoulder-length blond hair. With her, that's all it takes. Lily had added a rhinestone necklace to her ensemble, and Daisy had taken off her baseball cap. Laurel was wearing a baggy but clean chambray shirt . . . with a suspicious bulge in the pocket.

"Oh no, you don't," I told her. "Henry is not invited to my birthday dinner."

Laurel stood there acting wide-eyed and innocent, but Mom stared her down. Sheepishly Laurel stuck a hand in her shirt pocket, removing a small brown field mouse. Henry scampered up Laurel's arm to her shoulder as if he were about to make a nest in her hair.

"Out," I commanded, and Laurel disappeared.

"Why does she always carry that rodent around with her?" I asked.

Mom gave a gentle smile and said, "You know your sister doesn't make friends easily. Her animals are her friends."

"I wish she weren't so shy," I replied. "Why can't she be more normal?"

"I'm not shy," Lily put in.

"If she weren't shy, she wouldn't be Laurel," Daisy said, and my mother nodded.

Just then we heard Laurel washing her hands in the kitchen—thank goodness for antibacterial soap. When she returned, we all stood for a moment, admiring the table. There were candles and a vase of pink roses in the middle and a single white rose along with a small, gift-wrapped box next to my plate.

"Happy birthday, Rose," Mom said, smiling at me.

I smiled back, but as I pulled out my chair and sat down I knew the same sad feeling was settling over each of us. I miss Dad all the time, but there are moments when it hits me more that he's really gone. Dinner is the worst. Mom always sits at the foot of the table so she can zip into the kitchen; Daisy and Lily sit on one side, Laurel and I on the other. Which leaves the captain's chair at the head of the table empty.

I tried not to look at it.

Mom served the roast beef while Daisy passed the platter of potatoes and vegetables. Laurel buttered a roll, and Lily swished a straw around in her glass of chocolate milk. Everyone looked solemn. No one spoke.

"Hey, this is a party," I reminded them, trying to sound cheerful. I tasted the roast beef. "It's delicious," I said. "Thanks for going to so much trouble, Mom. I really didn't expect it."

"This is a special day. Nothing can change that," she replied, but this time when she smiled, I could tell it took an effort.

I did my best to keep the conversation hopping. It wasn't all that hard because Daisy and Lily both like to gab, and if you bring up the right topic, Laurel can, too.

"How was school, Toad?" I asked, using the nickname I gave her when she was six and spent the whole summer collecting slimy things in mason jars. "Did you finish your biology project?"

"We finished it today. Last week we fed the caterpillars all these leaves," Laurel reported, "and then they made chrysalides. Well, today the butterflies started to come out! It was so amazing. Next week we're doing tadpoles."

"How appropriate," I said. "Sounds perfect for you." She smiled and stared down at her plate.

"Ask me about my day!" Lily urged me.

"Okay, how was your day, Lily?"

"I did my book report on *Pippi Longstocking* and got an Excellent!"

"That's wonderful!" Mom told her. "Congratulations." Lily beamed.

I laughed. "Now I get it. That's what the pigtails are for, right?"

Lily nodded, pleased with herself. "I acted my report out for the class. All the girls in my class said they wished they'd thought of it. The only person whose report was half as good as mine was Amanda Waterston's, and you could tell that her mother helped her make her shadow box."

"It's better to do all the work yourself," I told her. "Good job."

"Maybe I can go to Wildwood next year," Lily said. "For acting! I'll be old enough."

"That would be great," I replied warmly. "I'd love to take you with me, Lily. It's so much fun, but I missed you guys last year." We grinned at each other a moment, then I looked at Daisy. "Okay, Daisy, your turn."

Daisy had already eaten a humongous slice of roast beef and was now halfway through her second serving of mashed potatoes. She paused just long enough to say, "Softball practice was canceled—Coach was sick. I wish that I had someone to play catch with when I can't practice with the team." Daisy's been a star athlete since toddlerhood, but the rest of us just aren't interested in sports.

"Have any of you girls met the new boy who's moved into Windy Ridge?" Mom wanted to know. Windy Ridge is the big old house at the end of Lighthouse Road—it's been vacant for almost a year. We all shook our heads. "Maybe he's interested in sports, Daisy."

"I don't know. I've seen him around—he seems too young to me," Daisy said. "He looks around Laurel's age."

"Maybe *you* could go introduce yourself, Laurel," Mom said.

Laurel flushed slightly.

"But you don't have to," Mom added hastily. Laurel looked relieved.

When we finished eating, Daisy cleared the table, then brought in clean plates for dessert.

"Before we cut the cake, why don't you open your gift, Rose?" Mom suggested.

That was the only invitation I needed. I'd been dying to tear into the wrapping paper but didn't want to seem too eager. Reminding myself that I was sixteen, not six, I opened the box with painstaking slowness. "Hurry up, Rose!" Lily said, but I just glared at her. I wondered what the gift would be. We've never been rich, but I had always dreamed that there would be a brand-new car in the driveway with a bow on top of it for my sixteenth birthday. Even though I knew it wasn't very likely, I couldn't help hoping briefly that the small box held a set of car keys.

But when I saw what was lying on a puff of cotton inside, I gasped. "Mom, it's beautiful!"

Everyone leaned in for a look. I held up the necklace so my sisters could admire it: a tiny gold rosebud suspended from a gold chain so delicate it was nearly invisible. "The rose was on your great-grandmother Walker's charm bracelet," my mother explained.

I fastened the clasp around my neck, then jumped up and ran to look at myself in the mirror over the sideboard. I loved what I saw. The necklace was pretty against my skin—just what the new dress needed. It might not be keys to my dream car, but I loved it.

Returning to the table, I wrapped my arms around my mother. "This is really a treasure. Thanks, Mom," I whispered.

We both had tears in our eyes. Mom hid hers by rising to her feet and disappearing into the kitchen. "Cake time," she called. "Dim the lights, Daisy, would you?"

As my mom carried the chocolate cake into the dining room Laurel ran into the living room to thump out an extremely off-key rendition of "Happy Birthday to You" on the piano. (I got all the musical talent in this family.) As everybody sang along Mom set the cake in front of me. Lily clapped, urging, "Make a wish!"

I drew in a breath, preparing to blow out the candles. *I wish . . . I wish Dad were still alive.*

Oh, God, what kind of birthday wish is that? I thought, shocked at myself. No matter how much I wanted it, there was no point wishing for something that couldn't possibly come true. I couldn't wish away the unexpected nor'easter that had swamped my father's fishing boat. I couldn't wish Dad back again. *If only I could.*

Shaking my head, I tried to come up with something else. Luckily for impatient Lily, another wish, one relating to my new boyfriend, Parker Kemp, and the possibility that someday my initials might be R. W. K., came quickly to mind.

I smiled and blew out the candles on my birthday cake—all sixteen of them at once.

Half an hour later I'd put on some makeup and perfume and brushed out my long blond hair, ready to head out the door as soon as Parker rang the bell. I stopped on my way past the kitchen.

The dishwasher was humming, the counters were spotless; even the blue-and-white-checked dish towels were hanging neatly from their pegs by the window. That's my mom—neat to a fault. But the drop-leaf table in the breakfast nook . . .

"Mom, what are you doing?" I asked.

She was sitting with her shoulders hunched forward, gnawing on a pencil. The table was piled high with file folders, checkbooks, and shoe boxes full of paper scraps.

Mom poked at the buttons on a calculator with the eraser end of a pencil, then glanced up at me distractedly. "Our income tax return," she answered. "I filed an extension last month, but I can't put it off indefinitely."

I wrinkled my nose. "Is it complicated?"

She sighed. "I loved your dad, but he was not a businessman. He left the finances in a mess. I can't make heads or tails of any of it."

"Well, don't stay up too late," I advised.

"Don't forget you have a curfew," she replied.

"I won't. Night, Mom."

Outside, I sat on the top porch step, hugging my knees and humming an Indigo Girls song. When a pair of headlights bumped down the gravel driveway, I stood up, my heart pounding with anticipation.

Whenever I go out with Parker, I feel like I'm entering a fairy tale. He whisks me into a different world.

He stepped out of his black Jeep Wrangler, leaving the engine running. Before helping me up into the passenger seat, he bent me back slightly against the side of the Jeep for a kiss. "Hey, birthday girl," he murmured, his mouth smiling against mine. "Nice dress."

It's hard to explain the effect Parker has on me, I mean without resorting to clichés like he makes my knees weak and all that. He looks like a Ralph Lauren model—blond hair and blue eyes and the kind of smile that stops you in your tracks. He's tall, too—six-foot one—with a lean, muscular tennis player's build. At the risk of sounding totally conceited, I have to say we look great together. Not that I'm obsessed with appearances or anything, but he's the first Seagate Academy guy I've gone out with, and that's kind of a status thing in Hawk Harbor.

"Do you know what day this is, besides my birthday?" I asked.

He scratched his head, pretending he didn't. "No, what?"

"It's our one-month anniversary," I reminded him, pinching his ribs playfully.

His face broke into a grin. "Of course I remember. I'll never forget the first time I saw you," Parker said.

I smiled up at him a little wistfully. I'd been feeling really sad about Dad that day, so I'd gone for a walk along the shore. That's where I feel closest to Dad because he spent so much time out on the ocean. I started walking at the public beach, too busy crying to pay attention to where I was going. I just kept climbing across rocks and jumping over tide pools and slogging through piles of seaweed as if I could somehow walk off my grief. Suddenly Parker had appeared before me.

"You looked so beautiful, but so sad," Parker went on.

I'd been kind of blown away when Parker told me we were standing on his family's private beach—that he lived in the mansion on the cliff above us. Maybe that was why, when I told him my father had died in a boating accident, I'd left out the fact that Dad had been a commercial fisherman. Of course, I'm sure that Parker could tell we weren't the kind of family that would have a yacht, but he never asked what kind of boat it was. And I never enlightened him.

Now I sniffled, feeling sentimental. A month ago on the rainy beach Parker had put an arm around me and pulled me under his umbrella. We'd been inseparable ever since. "I'm the luckiest girl in the world," I whispered softly.

"You're the prettiest girl in the world," said Parker, kissing me.

"So, where are we going?" I asked a minute later as Parker backed out of the driveway.

He gave me a sideways glance, smiling. "You'll see."

I settled back in my seat with a happy sigh. Parker has his own charge card, and he always takes me to pretty nice places. So I wasn't surprised when he pulled up in front of the Harborside. But I was surprised when he led me through the restaurant to a private room in the back. A room packed with kids wearing party hats who threw confetti into the air and shouted, "Surprise!"

I blinked. "What on . . . is this for . . . ?"

"Yep, it's for you," Parker said. "Happy birthday!"

Sliding an arm around my waist, he steered me into the crowd. I couldn't get over it. It wasn't just that Parker had thrown me a surprise party. It was a surprise party with armfuls of red roses in crystal vases all over the place, and a waiter passing a tray of hors d'oeuvres, and a two-tiered cake garnished with real rosebuds on a silver pedestal. It was a far cry from my fifteenth birthday party, which had consisted of pizzas and pitchers of Pepsi with my now ex-boyfriend Sully and other friends at the Rusty Nail, a very casual hangout in town.

"You really shouldn't have done this," I said to Parker, feeling a little embarrassed.

He shrugged as if it were nothing. "Come on, I want you to meet everybody."

We made a quick tour of the room. I mostly just smiled, trying to remember names—Chip van Alder, Cynthia Ferris, David Shuman, Valerie Mathias—and trying not to panic over the fact that I was the only girl in the room wearing a cotton dress. I took mental notes for future reference, not that I could afford to copy these girls' outfits. Seagate Academy girls obviously didn't shop the sale rack at Harrington's.

"Here." Parker pressed a glass of punch into my hand. "Be right back."

For a minute I stood alone by the buffet table, sipping my punch. It seemed a little strange—here I was at my own birthday party with no one to talk to. I edged up to a conversation. "So if I can score some tickets, maybe we could road trip to Boston for the concert," David was saying.

"What concert?" I asked brightly.

"We could crash at my cousin's dorm," Cynthia went on, as if she hadn't heard me. She was looking from David to Chip. "If we stay over Saturday, we could go to some Harvard parties."

"I don't want to miss the crew regatta, though," Chip told Cynthia. "What if we—"

They didn't seem to need me, so I backed up a step or two. "I think I'll have some cake," I said to no one in particular. I looked around for Parker, but he was on the far side of the room, talking to Valerie. "Yes, it's cake time," I decided, turning to the buffet.

As I contemplated the cake someone behind me said, "It's almost too beautiful to cut."

I glanced over my shoulder at a tall guy with deep brown eyes. He had thick, dark hair and small wire-rimmed glasses. He looked like a future professor in spite of the fact that he was incredibly handsome.

"Yes," I agreed, feeling a little ridiculous about the fact that this person was at my party and I had no idea who he was. I turned back to the cake. Oh, well, I thought. Let them eat—

"Cake," the guy said.

"What?" I asked.

"Let them eat cake," he repeated. "I'm sure the chef would hate to think that he went to all the trouble of making it taste good for nothing."

"You have a point," I said. Smiling, I grabbed the silver knife on the table and sliced into the cake. I offered him the first piece. "By the way, I'm Rose," I said.

"Sorry. I should have introduced myself sooner." He actually blushed. "Stephen Mathias," he said as we shook hands.

"Mathias. Then you must be Valerie's"—I inspected him more closely. Valerie is the same age as Parker and me, sixteen, and a sophomore. This guy looked a little older—"big brother?"

"Right," he said. "I'm a junior."

I don't usually have trouble talking to people, but this guy was a little intimidating. He was staring at me kind of intensely, as if he was trying to figure something out, which was making me worry that maybe I had a blob of frosting on my face or something. I glanced around for Parker, hoping he'd rescue me. Suddenly Stephen remarked, "You don't go to Seagate, do you?" Now it was my turn to flush slightly. "I mean," he added quickly, "I'd remember seeing you around."

"No, I go to South Regional," I admitted, naming my public high school. It was pretty obvious that I didn't fit in with this crowd, and I hated the fact that it bothered me so much.

"Well." He rocked back on his heels. "This is quite a party."

I nodded. "Unbelievable."

"It was a surprise, huh?" he asked. I couldn't read the look on his face.

I nodded again.

"So, where are your friends?"

"I wouldn't have expected Parker to invite people he's never met," I said a little defensively.

"You two haven't been dating that long, then?"

"Well, a month, but—" I stopped, frowning. A whole month and Parker still hadn't met my best friends. Why not?

At that moment someone who smelled like expensive men's cologne came up behind me and wrapped his arms around my waist. "Don't eat too much cake," Parker murmured, his lips on my earlobe.

I put my plate down fast and turned to face him. "Ready for your present?" he asked.

"You mean this party isn't my present?"

"Of course not."

He pressed a robin's egg blue box into my hand. "For me?"

Parker laughed. "Who else? Open it."

Stephen had drifted away, but Cynthia and a few other girls crowded around to watch. I heard Valerie say, "That's a Tiffany box." Self-conscious, I opened it. When I saw what was inside, I almost fainted. I lifted out the heavy silver necklace.

"Parker," I whispered, "it's lovely."

Removing the necklace my mother had given me earlier in the evening, Parker fastened the clasp of the Tiffany one around my neck. "Now, that does you justice," he said, bending forward to kiss me. "You're so beautiful. I love you, Rose."

It was the first time he'd said that. My eyes widened in surprise, but I closed them as our lips touched. Parker Kemp loved me!

Our kiss went on and on. Parker's friends clapped and whistled, but we still didn't draw apart.

Fifteen had been a terrible year—I'd lost my father. The year I turned sixteen was bound to be better. One thing's for sure, I thought, dizzy with happiness. It's off to a great start.

In the middle of the night something woke me up. For a few seconds I lay with my eyes closed, trying to get back into the dream I'd been having. It was about Parker, of course. Then I heard the sound again. "Daddy!" someone cried. "Daddy, come here!"

Lily, I thought groggily. My youngest sister has a seriously overactive imagination—she has nightmares all the time, and Dad's the only one who can calm her down. I lay in the dark, waiting for the sound of his footsteps plodding down the hall. Lily kept crying, "Daddy, I'm scared!"

A minute passed, then two, and I was starting to wonder what was taking Dad so long.

And then I remembered.

Hopping out of bed, I hurried to Lily's room. She was sitting up in bed, a pillow clutched to her chest and tears sliding down her face. I sat down on the mattress and put an arm around her, wondering what to say. "It's okay," I murmured.

"Where's Daddy? I want Daddy," Lily sobbed.

I wished I didn't have to tell her the truth. "Dad's not here," I reminded her at last, "and Mom's still asleep. She was really tired tonight."

Lily sagged against me, her head on my shoulder.

Her tears wouldn't stop. "I had this awful dream, Rose," she whispered, sniffling. "I was wading in Kettle Cove looking for clams and this big shark swam up and I . . ."

As Lily went on, I could feel her still shaking with fear. What had Dad done in this situation? I wondered, feeling helpless. I wasn't used to playing this role.

"There, there," I murmured.

Lily kept crying. I was totally at a loss. Help me, Dad, I thought.

Dad always believed in being as rational as possible. I took a deep breath. "It'll be okay. There aren't any sharks in Kettle Cove."

Lily looked up at me. "There aren't?" she asked with another sniff.

"Definitely not," I declared. "They like the beaches down on Cape Cod. In fact, they prefer . . ." and I went off on some long, rambling explanation that was half remembered from an old science textbook and half invention.

Believe it or not, it worked. I held Lily until her eyelids drooped sleepily. Then I tucked her back in.

As I was closing the door Lily woke up again. "Where are you going?" she asked.

"Back to my room," I said.

She thought about this for a minute.

"I'll be right down the hall," I added.

"Okay," she said. "Thanks, Rose."

Oh, Dad, I thought, what was it you used to say? "Anytime," I whispered.

Two

"Stop making me laugh," Catherine Appleby begged Sumita Ghosh as we headed out of school the next day after concert choir. "Or I'll wet my pants."

Mita had been mimicking the way Mr. Arnold, the music director at South Regional High, instructs the sopranos by singing their parts in this quavery falsetto. It was hilarious. Mita's from India. She has this totally cool British accent, but she can imitate anyone.

Cath was doubled over. She did look close to losing it, so Mita took pity on her. "Okay," Mita said, putting one arm around me and the other around Roxanne Beale. She started belting out the raunchy lyrics to a rock song. We all joined in at the top of our lungs—it felt great after an hour and a half of practicing prim songs for the spring concert. People call us the "Fab Four" because there are four of us and we're always singing.

"Who needs a ride?" Cath asked when we got to the student parking lot. She jingled the keys to her father's blue Dodge pickup.

I dropped my book bag on the sidewalk, then

took a seat on the curb. "Not me," I replied. "Parker's picking me up."

"Ooh." Rox wriggled her light eyebrows. She has strawberry blond hair and is very fair. "Parker."

"The man," teased Cath, her green eyes sparkling.

"Did Prince Charming make your birthday extra special?" Mita asked suggestively.

I rolled my eyes. "As a matter of fact, he did. He threw this amazing party at the . . ." I remembered Parker's oversight and stopped, embarrassed. "I wish you guys could have been there, but it was a pretty small party, actually," I finished lamely. "Low-key. We didn't even dance."

"Hey, no big deal," Rox assured me.

"He doesn't even know us," Cath pointed out.

"We want to do something for you, though," Mita said, "to celebrate."

"How about Pizza Bowl?" Cath suggested. "We'll round up everybody this Friday night."

"We could invite Parker," Rox added charitably.

I tried to picture Parker at the bowling alley, munching a slice of pepperoni with extra cheese, but my imagination couldn't stretch that far. "Um, I'll ask him, but I think he's going away this weekend," I improvised. Parker's family has a house in Boston, too, so it wasn't hard to come up with a story. "Yeah, I'm pretty sure he'll be in Boston."

To my relief, they dropped the topic and we moved on to our favorite joke fantasy: forming an all-girl singing group after we graduate in two years. Mita put forth her argument for opening our first set with a Rolling Stones cover.

We decided to try it out and started singing "Start Me Up"—Mita even threw in some Mick Jagger moves. Just then a black Jeep pulled into the parking lot. Abruptly the husky musical notes died in my throat. I jumped to my feet, one hand flying up to smooth my hair, the other quickly flicking the dirt off the seat of my jeans. The grunge look is cool in some circles, but not at Seagate Academy. Parker always looks totally crisp, as if his clothes get dry-cleaned—with him in them.

I grabbed my bag, swinging it over my shoulder, and started toward the Jeep. Then I turned back. "Come over and meet Parker," I said to my friends, who didn't need to be asked twice— they'd been dying to meet Parker. It was about time, wasn't it?

I strode over to the driver's side of the Jeep with Cath, Mita, and Rox at my heels. "Parker, hey." I gave him a quick kiss. "These are my friends. Cath Appleby—you know Appleby's Hardware in town? And Roxanne—her dad used to . . ." I caught myself before saying "her dad used to fish with my dad." For some reason I didn't want Parker to know that. "Her dad's a fisherman," I went on, "and Mita's parents run that really excellent Indian restaurant in Eastport."

Rox, Mita, and Cath took turns shaking Parker's hand, as if he were fifty years old or something. Parker gave them a smile, but it wasn't his usual turn-your-bones-to-butter smile. Why is this weird? I wondered. Did I say something wrong?

"Nice to meet you," Parker said.

"Nice to meet you, too," Mita, Rox, and Cath replied.

An awkward silence fell over us. "Yeah, the Bombay Palace," I went on in an attempt to jumpstart the conversation. "Have you ever eaten there, Parker?"

"Haven't had the pleasure," Parker said.

I faltered. "Well. Um . . ."

"Hop in," Parker suggested. "Nice to meet you," he said to my friends.

I got into the passenger seat, confused and disappointed. So there hadn't been instant chemistry between Parker and my girlfriends. So what? When they get to know one another better, it'll be cool, I told myself.

"See ya," I called out the window to Cath, Rox, and Mita.

"See ya," they replied, waving as Parker and I drove off.

Parker and I went to the Seagate library and then out for a snack. It was six o'clock when he dropped me off at the house. Mom was just putting dinner on the table. "Will you join us, Parker?" she invited, smiling at him from the dining room.

We were still standing in the front hall. "It's just stew, but my mom's is the best," I whispered.

Parker checked his watch in a kind of exaggerated

way—stretching out his arm, then bringing his hand back in with the wrist cocked. "I really need to get home," he told me. "Can't, but thanks, anyway, Mrs. Walker," he called.

After Parker left, I took my place at the table. Lily, Laurel, and Daisy were already in their chairs, rattling silverware and reaching for the serving bowls and platters. I piled my plate high; I was starving. Parker and I had stopped at a coffee shop in town, but I hadn't wanted to seem like a pig— I'd just ordered a diet soda.

"Parker never hangs out here," Daisy remarked, buttering a corn muffin.

"Yeah, well . . ." I considered this statement. It was true. "He has . . . lots of things to do."

"Is his house more fun or something?" asked Lily.

I thought about Parker's house: the awesome CD and video collection, the big-screen TV, the pool, the sauna. It was more fun. Before I could answer Lily's question, though, Laurel said, "I guess he doesn't have to talk to us if he doesn't want to."

I looked at Mom, wondering what she thought about all this. That's when I noticed that five minutes into the meal, she hadn't touched her food. "Are you feeling okay, Mom?" I asked.

Mom propped her elbows on the table, chin on clasped hands. Her blue eyes were somber. "I need to talk to you girls about something," she said, "but I don't know where to start."

"What is it?" Daisy asked.

Mom paused before speaking. "It's about our . . . finances."

"Finances?" Lily repeated, puzzled.

"That means money," Daisy told Lily.

"What about our finances?" I asked.

"Your father had a life insurance policy, but it was small," Mom began. "It covered his funeral expenses, some old debts from the fishing business, and a couple of household bills. That's all."

"But you have a job now, Mom," said Daisy. "And we've been economizing. Right?"

I scowled at the word *economizing*. That's what we'd been doing since Dad died, and it wasn't fun. Economizing meant spaghetti for dinner every other night. It meant no renting videos and no more going out for pizza and ice cream on Friday nights like we did when Dad was alive. No new clothes, no new anything.

"I have a job," Mom agreed. She worked at a local real estate agency, answering phones and filing. I knew she felt lucky to have landed the position—she and my father married young, and she never went to college. Being a mom had always taken all her time. "But I'm still only part-time, and my salary doesn't come close to meeting our expenses. The upkeep on the house—food—utilities—taxes . . ."

Mom stopped. The four of us girls sat quietly, waiting. Where was all this leading?

"We'll be all right," she said at last. "We'll pull through. I'm trying to get more hours at work. But

in the short-term I'm going to have to apply for . . .
assistance."

Daisy tipped her head to one side. Laurel and
Lily exchanged a confused glance. A sick feeling
bubbled in my stomach. Maybe my sisters didn't
know what Mom meant by *assistance*, but I did.
Welfare, I thought numbly.

"Couldn't we ask Gram and Gramps for money?"
Daisy said.

Mom's parents retired to Florida—my other
grandparents are both dead. "No," Mom answered
Daisy. "Grampa's pension from the telephone
company is barely enough for the two of them."

I opened my mouth to ask if the bank could
lend us some money. Mom turned to me at the
same instant and spoke first. "Rose, I've been
meaning to talk to you about Wildwood."

A chill ran over my entire body.

"I know how much you love it," she went on. I
nodded, unable to speak.

Mom chewed her lower lip. "The thing is,
honey," she said apologetically, "camp counselors
don't get paid much. Hardly anything, really. And
now that you're sixteen . . ."

I stared at her for a minute before putting into
words what she obviously couldn't bring herself to
say. "You want me to give up Wildwood and find
some other job that pays more?" I asked, although
it wasn't really a question.

"It's your choice," Mom hurried to assure me.
"But whatever you do, you'll need to start putting

money aside for college. I won't be able to cover your clothing allowance anymore, either, or your spending money. I know this is hard for you, Rose."

My sisters were gaping at me. I looked down at my plate, my jaw clenched. I was fighting back tears. Wildwood was the best part of the entire year. It was my only chance to study with people who knew about music and performance. I remembered how excited I'd been when I got the letter from the camp director offering me the job. Right away I'd called Julianne Greenberg, my camp friend from Connecticut. She'd gotten a letter, too, and we'd talked for an hour about how much fun this summer was going to be.

I knew that I shouldn't take it so hard, but I couldn't help it.

"I'll look for a job in town," I managed to say after a minute that felt like a month.

"I'm sorry, honey," Mom said. "I really am."

"Excuse me, I'm not hungry anymore," I mumbled, pushing back my chair. Turning my head so no one would see the tears that were flowing down my face, I hurried from the table.

"No, that's not right." I shifted the key from major to minor, humming as I played.

It was a rainy afternoon a week after Mom broke the bad news about going on welfare, and I was sitting at the piano trying to write a song for Parker. I wanted it to be upbeat, obviously, a song about being madly in love, but the words and notes kept coming out gloomy. I'd been feeling down all week and—with the exception of the night my friends and I went to Pizza Bowl—it was a feeling I couldn't seem to shake. "It's a gray day and I'm missing you, wishing you were here," I sang. I scribbled a few notes on the composition pad on top of the piano, then scratched them out, making a sour face. "Blech!"

For a minute I sat with my hands flat on the bench beside me, staring out the rain-streaked window. Then my fingers moved back to the keys and began picking out a melody Natalie Merchant recorded back when she was with 10,000 Maniacs. "'Shiver in my bones just thinking about the weather,'" I sang softly.

With a sigh I gave up trying to be creative. Just as I was stowing my composition pad in the piano bench Laurel burst through the front door into the hall, her hair flying out behind her, Henry clutched in one hand. "Rose, someone's stealing our car!"

Her cry brought Daisy and Lily running from the kitchen. All four of us crowded over to the living room window. Sure enough, there was a tow truck parked in our driveway and a man in an orange mechanic's jumpsuit was attaching a cable to the bumper of our silver Buick, working fast because of the drizzle. Another man walked briskly up to the house. I met him at the door. "Here's the notice from your bank," he said, handing me a rain-spattered envelope. "Sorry, miss."

I closed and locked the door, then rejoined my

sisters. "They're not stealing it—they're repossessing it," I informed them.

"That's Dad's car," Daisy said angrily. "I'm going to tell them they can't take it!"

She started for the door. Leaping after her, I grabbed her arm. "Mom must not have been making the loan payments. Just chill, Daze."

"It's not fair," she said, her eyes still blazing.

"I know," I agreed.

We squeezed onto the couch, all four of us, and looked out the window in silence. Dad's car. Funny how we all still thought of it that way, even though Mom drove it and I did, too, now that I had my license. Dad's car.

I remembered the day we bought it, about a year before Dad died. He took us with him to the used car lot, and he acted as if he really cared about our opinions. "What do you think, Rose?" he'd asked me. "Does it look like a fisherman's car?"

"Nope," I'd replied.

He'd grinned, his blue eyes twinkling. "Good."

We went for a test drive. Dad put all the windows down and we cranked the oldies station, screaming along to the Beatles and Beach Boys. When we got back to the dealership, Dad told the used car guy, "You've made a sale." And we drove the car home.

Now I remembered asking Dad why he'd picked the Buick instead of a van or something more practical. "Don't get me wrong," he'd answered. "I'm not trying to be someone I'm not. I just want a nice car for my girls to ride in."

Now Daisy, Laurel, Lily, and I watched the tow truck rumble out of the driveway with the sedan rolling behind it. Daisy picked at the fringe on the crocheted afghan that hung over the back of the couch. "We really don't need two cars, anyway," she said.

Typical Daisy—always looking for the silver lining. No point reminding her that the only car we had left was an ancient and hideous wood-sided station wagon.

Laurel remained silent, cradling her pet mouse against her cheek. For once I felt too sorry for her— and for all of us—to be grossed out. Lily moved closer to me on the sofa. "What does 'repossessed' mean, Rose?" she asked, her eyes large with fear. "Will those men come back and take more things away?"

I put an arm around Lily without answering. I didn't know how to explain it to her. In my head, though, I ran over the meanings of the word. *Repossessed* meant we couldn't afford to make the payments. *Repossessed* meant we couldn't afford anything.

For days Mom, my sisters, and I had had one conversation after another about money, or rather the lack of it. Sacrifices we'd have to make. Lifestyle changes.

But that wasn't the worst of it. Hawk Harbor was a fishbowl—I bet at least a dozen people could see our car being towed and would immediately begin speculating why.

How long would it be before everyone in town found out?

Three

"Everyone's being so nice," Daisy said later that week. "Isn't everyone being nice?"

Saturdays have always been crazy at our house—everybody coming and going, friends in and out, umpteen projects under way. That Saturday was no exception. Daisy was just back from a softball tournament, Mom was washing and ironing curtains, Lily and her friends Mickey and Noelle were staging a play in the living room, and I was recovering. And Laurel was out on a rescue mission with her new friend, Jack Harrison.

Jack was the boy who had moved into Windy Ridge—I had been wondering whether we would ever meet him. When he rang our doorbell that morning, Laurel hid in her room while I answered the door. But Jack had come to tell "the girl who takes care of the animals" that he had found a nest of baby raccoons who needed care. He didn't know what to do. His young face was so serious that I immediately went upstairs and knocked on Laurel's door. Once she understood the situation, Laurel forgot her shyness and rushed downstairs. I expected them back with the raccoons any minute.

As if the house wasn't full enough already! Our neighbor Mr. Comiskey had dropped by to borrow a drill and had stayed to fix some loose shingles on the roof, "since I'm here." Old Mrs. Schenkel from two doors down had just dropped off a wheelbarrow full of canned goods, explaining that she and Mr. Schenkel were about to leave on a cruise and she was "cleaning out her cupboards."

Nineteen-year-old Stan Smith from two doors down in the other direction was at that very moment fixing a leaky tap in the upstairs bathroom. Stan's mother, Sue, who's a good friend of Mom's, had walked over with Stan to return a pie dish she'd borrowed "sometime in the previous century."

"And look!" Daisy whispered to me now. Daisy was putting the pie dish away while Mrs. Smith chatted with Mom on the porch. "There's money in here!"

I peered into the pie dish. Sure enough, along with some recipe cards there was a plain white envelope. It wasn't sealed, and when Daisy lifted the flap, we both could see the green bills. Daisy started to count it. "Stop," I exclaimed, snatching the envelope and the dish away from her. "Have some pride, would you?"

I stomped into the kitchen with the pie dish, setting it on the counter with a loud clunk. Then my curiosity got the better of me. I peeked into the envelope, rifling the bills quickly. Three fives, two tens, and a twenty. Fifty-five dollars! And the Smiths weren't exactly millionaires. Mr. Smith was the custodian at the grade school, and Mrs. Smith sold little jars of homemade jams and jellies through local gift stores. Stan was the oldest of five kids. So if they were giving money to us . . .

Charity, I thought, overcome by an unpleasant mixture of gratitude and shame. People always think about how hard it is to give, but they never think about how hard it is to receive.

The envelope of money turned out to be nothing compared to what we had to endure the following Monday afternoon. Mom, Daisy, and Lily picked me up after choral practice in the station wagon, which still smelled like fish because Dad used it to haul nets and equipment back and forth from the marina. "Just have to make one stop on the way home," Mom announced, turning onto Old Boston Post Road.

The county social services center is on a busy street, with a huge sign—you'd think they could have been more discreet. "This may take a while," Mom warned as she parked in a space right in front where anyone driving by could see us. "They told me on the phone that I'd have to fill out a bunch of forms."

She left the key in the ignition so we could listen to the radio. I tuned it to a rock station, then slumped down in the passenger seat so only the top of my head would be visible. Meanwhile in the backseat Daisy and Lily continued to sit up as straight as they could, gabbing on and on about some stupid book Lily's teacher was reading out loud to the third graders.

"So there's this tollbooth, but it's magic," Lily reported to Daisy.

"*The Phantom Tollbooth*," Daisy responded with enthusiasm. "I loved that one."

I wanted to yell at them to shut up. Didn't they know what was going on? Didn't they care? I knew it was a horrible thought, but I wanted to drive off, leaving Mom behind. Who needed food stamps, anyway? I'd rather just go on a diet.

I didn't yell, though, and I didn't drive off, and I didn't cry, which was something else I felt like doing. Instead I turned the radio up louder, folded my arms tightly across my chest, and closed my eyes.

"Why can't you wear the dress you wore to the homecoming dance with Sully?" Rox wanted to know on Wednesday.

Rox, Cath, Mita, and I had gone into town after school. I needed a dress for the Seagate Academy prom, but I had only eighteen dollars saved up. My friends were having diet soda and candy bars, but I had to do without since I didn't have a dime to spare. We strolled along the sidewalk, discussing my options.

Now that Memorial Day weekend had come and gone, Main Street was starting to wake up from its winter sleep. I paused in front of a new boutique called Cecilia's. "I went in there the other day— they have nice stuff," Cath commented.

"Expensive, though," Mita said.

I turned away from the window. What was the point of even looking? Cecilia's catered to the summer crowd and families like the Kemps—I couldn't afford to shop there.

"I can't wear my homecoming dress," I explained somewhat impatiently, "because it's last year's dress. Besides, it's not even the right season."

"Who'd know?" wondered Rox. "Nobody from Seagate's seen you in it, and it's sleeveless. It could be a spring dress."

"I can't wear it," I repeated firmly. "Besides, Sully spilled a Coke all over me. There's this huge stain on the skirt."

"You could borrow my yellow dress," offered Cath.

I had to smile at that. Cath's yellow dress is gorgeous. Cath, however, is the world's smallest person—I'm six inches taller than she is. "I like short dresses, but not that short," I said.

"Well, they're having another sale at Harrington's," Rox said.

I shook my head, sighing. Even at Harrington's, on sale, I couldn't afford a brand-new dress. That was all there was to it.

I was ready to give up. Then Mita said suddenly, "I've got an idea. Let's check out Second Time Around."

I glanced at her, one eyebrow lifted. "That's a consignment shop," I pointed out, picturing racks of tacky chiffon mother-of-the-bride dresses.

"They sell vintage clothing," Mita corrected

me in her precise and refined British manner. I continued to look skeptical. "I've found some funky things there," she pressed. "Trust me!"

I thought about it a minute. Oh, well. What could it hurt? I didn't have many options. "Okay, let's try it," I said.

At the next corner we turned down a side street, pausing to breathe in the delicious smell of Wissinger's Bakery. Second Time Around was halfway down the block.

It was a mild day, and the door to the store was propped open. Cowboy Junkies' version of "Sweet Jane" wafted out to the sidewalk, along with the smell of incense. Maybe this won't be so horrible after all, I thought hopefully.

Mita yanked me straight to a rack in the back. "How about this?" She pulled out a dress. "Or this?"

Cath and Rox pounced on the dresses. "Oh, I like this one," Cath said. "Check out the lace."

"How about this?" Rox grabbed a hanger with something psychedelic on it. "It's kind of seventies. *Mod Squad*, you know? Groovy, baby."

I started to get excited in spite of myself. I studied the first dress Mita had picked out. "I love the color," I said. "What would you call it, olive?"

"Sage," Mita said. She held the dress against me. "It's perfect for you. And it's only . . ." She flicked the price tag in my direction. It had been marked down a couple of times. I could afford the dress and still have enough cash left over to buy a boutonniere for Parker.

I looked at my reflection in the mirror. "I'm trying it on," I declared.

I marched to the dressing room with Mita, Cath, and Rox trailing in my wake. The four of us crowded behind the curtain together. Their faces were intent as I stripped out of my short denim skirt and T-shirt and pulled the dress over my head.

Choosing a prom dress is serious business.

When the dress was on, though, they all melted. "Oh, Rose, you look beautiful," Cath gushed.

Rox sighed. "It's romantic."

"Parker's eyes will pop out of his head," Mita predicted.

A blush of pleasure stole across my cheeks as I looked at myself in the mirror. The dress was simple and a little bit old-fashioned, but that was what made it flattering. The soft fabric fell straight, tucking in just slightly at the waist, the hem hitting me midcalf. The wide, scooped neckline was edged in lace, as were the sheer elbow-length sleeves. "The woman who first wore this dress is probably a grandma by now," I said with a laugh.

"A sexy grandma," Mita said. "I think you look hot." Her dark eyes sparkled. "Didn't I tell you we'd hit the jackpot here?"

I don't have a problem admitting when I'm wrong. "You were right, O Wise One," I said, grinning.

Mita, Cath, and Rox left so I could change back into my own clothes. First I twirled in front of the mirror, enjoying the way the delicate fabric draped against my body. Then I stopped, a frown creasing my forehead. We'd all agreed the dress was perfect—or was it? Something's not right, I thought. Was it the length? The neckline?

Then I focused on the necklace I was wearing—my birthday gift from Parker. That was the problem, definitely. I wanted to wear the necklace on prom night, but it looked odd with the dress—too ornate. Too Tiffany. Is that possible? I wondered, gnawing my lip.

For a millisecond I considered returning the dress to the rack. Then I shook my head. No, I loved the necklace, but I loved the dress, too. Besides, I could wear the necklace anytime.

After changing fast, I hurried to the cash register with the dress slung over my arm.

Parker picked me up at my house after dinner that night. We'd made plans to study together at the town library—finals were coming up—but somehow we found ourselves parked at the beach. "And what do you know," said Parker, grinning at me in the twilight. "There's a blanket in the back of the Jeep."

"How do you suppose that got there?" I asked, pretending to be shocked.

Leaving our shoes behind, we walked across the cool sand, aiming for a sheltered spot in the dunes. The sun had just set behind us; ahead, the purple sky over the ocean was beginning to sparkle with stars.

Parker spread the blanket and flopped down on

it. I stretched out beside him, anticipating a long, warm, wonderful kiss. Instead he stayed away from me, propping himself up on one elbow. "So, are things okay at home?" he asked out of the blue.

"Sure," I said, surprised. "Why do you ask?"

"I just heard something about how, like, maybe money's a little bit tight since your dad passed away." His hand traced circles in the sand.

What had he heard? I wondered. A vague rumor or gory details? I acted casual, hoping it was the former. "Yeah, money's tight, but we're managing. My mom's got a pretty good job." I should have stopped there, but I didn't. The lies began slipping out before I could stop myself. "I mean, it's not the same without Dad. Like, the Buick broke down and Mom had no idea what to do so she had it towed someplace and who knows when we'll get it back. But you don't have to worry about us," I declared. "It turns out my dad had this big insurance policy. So everything's"—*awful. Terrifying*—"fine."

"Glad to hear it," Parker said, visibly relieved.

I redirected the conversation fast. "I'm so excited about the prom, Parker. I've never been to one! Is it just sophomores? Where is it going to be?"

"Rocky Point Country Club," he replied. "All four classes together—it's a small school. Hey, by the way, have you bought a dress yet? I need to know the color so I can order a corsage to match."

"I did buy a dress," I told him. "It's really pretty, but the color's kind of hard to describe. I'll show it to you when you drop me off."

We kissed for a while, but for some reason I couldn't relax. I kept thinking about the lies I'd told Parker. He'd asked me a straightforward question—why hadn't I been honest?

When it started to get cold at the beach, we went to the library. It was about ten when Parker took me home. I brought him inside, and we stuck our heads into the family room to say hi to Mom, who was watching the news. "I'm just going to show Parker my new dress," I told her.

"Okay. How was the library?" Mom asked.

"Full of books," Parker replied, giving my waist a secret little pinch. Then he pointed to the news program on the TV. "Anything interesting happening in the real world, Mrs. Walker?"

"The usual madness and mayhem," she replied.

"You got to love it, though, just for the contrast," Parker said. "Hawk Harbor can be pretty slow. If my family didn't have a place in Boston, we'd go nuts."

A funny expression flickered across Mom's face. Parker's right—Hawk Harbor can be boring—but it's also home. Mom's lived here all her life. "Show Parker that dress, Rose," Mom suggested. "I think he'll like it."

We stepped back into the hall.

"The dress is in my closet," I told Parker.

"Are you inviting me to your bedroom?" he kidded.

"Sure, with the lights on and the door open and my sisters right next door."

Upstairs, I pulled the dress from my closet, holding it against my body so Parker could admire it properly. "It's kind of green," I said. "Sage. Probably just about any color corsage would—" I noticed his expression and stopped. "The dress looks really pretty on," I assured him.

"Maybe," he said without conviction. "Rose, though, the thing is, the Seagate prom is really . . . formal."

For a moment I didn't know what to say. "You think this dress isn't nice enough?" I asked, crestfallen.

"I want you to have fun at the dance, that's all," he said. He took the dress and tossed it onto the bed, then gave me a hug. "I want you to feel like you fit in. And you're such a knockout. You should be wearing something more . . ." He stepped back, snapping his fingers. "I bet Val has a dress you could borrow."

"Val?" I repeated.

"Valerie Mathias—you met her at your birthday party. She has a closet full of formal stuff."

"How do you know?" I asked crabbily, folding my arms across my chest.

Parker smiled. "I confess—I've been in her room. We used to go out, kind of on-again, off-again."

"Oh, I see," I said, though I wasn't sure that I did.

"Anyhow, I'll take care of it. You'll be perfect— the prettiest girl at the prom," Parker promised, pulling me to him for a kiss.

The prettiest girl at the prom, I mused a little while later as I walked back upstairs. I'd seen Parker out to his car and we'd kissed again and I'd decided to be grateful for his offer to get a dress for me instead of insulted, which had been my first response. Hadn't he said he was just thinking about my feelings? I frowned. If that was the case, then how come my feelings were hurt?

For about the thousandth time since he died, I wished I could talk to my father. It had never seemed quite right, dating a boy Dad hadn't checked out first. I remembered his assessment of Sully a couple of years ago. "Nice boy, but he's not as bright as you." Dad had grinned. "Which is okay in the romantic department. Your mother's twice as smart as I am."

Would Dad have liked Parker? I wondered, trying unsuccessfully to imagine the two of them having a guy-to-guy chat about football or cars. Okay, so maybe it wouldn't have been love at first sight. But Dad was a generous, tolerant person, I thought. He would see Parker's good qualities—how smart he was, and how much he liked me.

How about Parker? It was hard to guess what he'd have thought about Dad since I never discussed Dad with him. Why is that? I asked myself. Am I afraid he'll look down on me or something since my dad was a fisherman and his dad's a stockbroker?

Still thinking about Dad, I headed down the hall to the bathroom to brush my teeth. I passed

Daisy's room—it was dark, and so were Lily's and Laurel's rooms. When I heard a muffled noise, though, I stopped.

Was Lily having another bad dream?

Then I realized the sound had come from Laurel's room. "Toad?" I called quietly. "Are you all right?"

She didn't answer, but I heard the telltale sound again and I pushed open the door. Laurel was sitting up in bed, her hair even more tangled than usual. I sat next to her. "What's the matter, Toad? Why are you crying?"

She pressed her face against my shoulder, her body shaking with quiet sobs. "I miss Daddy." She looked up at me, her eyes bright with tears. "I miss him so much. Don't you, Rose?"

I nodded, my own throat suddenly tight with tears. "Yes," I told her. "I do."

Four

Valerie dropped the dress off on Saturday. It was possibly the most embarrassing moment of my life. "Parker said you needed a dress for the prom," she said, pulling a dry cleaner's bag out of the backseat of her black Saab. "I hope this fits. You're a little bigger than me."

We were standing in my driveway. I took the bag, feeling ridiculous. "Uh, do you want to come in? Have a soda or something?"

"Can't." She glanced over her shoulder at my house. I saw it through her eyes—old and somewhat dilapidated. "Thanks, anyway."

"Thank you. For the dress."

Valerie climbed back behind the wheel of the car. "Just clean it before you give it back, okay?"

"Sure."

She flashed a smile before she drove away. "See you at the prom, Rose."

I went inside, holding the hanger high so the dress wouldn't trail on the ground. The house rumbled around me, buzzing with Saturday sounds: Daisy vacuuming, Lily and Laurel squabbling, a distant radio tuned to the classical music station Mom likes.

In my room I pulled the dry cleaner's bag off Valerie's dress. Now that I could really see it, I caught my breath. It was gorgeous. The strapless bodice was made of light blue satin, and the poofy short skirt was soft ivory. I'll wear high heels, pale stockings, and the silver necklace from Parker, I thought excitedly.

I fingered the expensive fabric, imagining myself wearing the dress as I danced with Parker at the Seagate Academy prom. With this dress I would be the prettiest girl there. Parker was right.

Then my happy smile faded. Something was bothering me . . . but what? Was it the idea that the dress somehow mattered more than I did? That in a plainer dress, a secondhand dress, I'd be less attractive, less important, less special?

My gaze shifted to the closet, where the sage green vintage dress from Second Time Around was hanging. Then I looked back at the blue-and-ivory dress. "Don't you want to be beautiful?" I asked myself.

I was yawning over my cereal bowl on Monday morning when my mother flew through the kitchen, her heels clattering. A car horn honked outside in the driveway. "That's my ride," she said, sticking her arms in the sleeves of a blazer as she hurried to the door. "You can take the wagon today. Would you pick Daisy up after softball? And stop at the grocery store on the way home—there's a list on the counter. Thanks a million, honey."

I rinsed out my bowl, then stuck it in the dishwasher. I still had to brush my teeth and get my books together, and by the time I was ready to head out to the car, I'd almost forgotten about the grocery list. I doubled back to get it.

The list was on the counter as Mom had said, but it wasn't alone. Right next to it was a book of food stamp coupons.

Having my driver's license is a mixed blessing, I decided, eyeing the food stamps with distaste. When I got my license, I was so psyched to cruise around town that I'd volunteered to do errands. I wished I could take back the offer, but it was too late. I hesitated for a second, then picked up the coupons gingerly, shoving them as far down in my book bag as possible.

At school I hid the food stamps in my locker, figuring out of sight, out of mind. Instead I couldn't stop thinking about them. By lunch period I'd decided to talk to my friends about my dilemma. Maybe Rox knows about this kind of stuff, I speculated. After all, Mr. Beale had been unemployed for a while a few years back. And what about Sumita's family, when they first got to the United States from India, before the restaurant took off?

The four of us staked out our usual table, near the vending machines by the back wall of the cafeteria. We opened our lunches—we'd all brought from home—and everyone else began eating. I took my time unwrapping my sandwich, considering how to bring up the food stamps. Before I could, though, Mita gestured with a carrot stick. "So, we're all waiting to hear about The Dress!" she declared, giving the words capital letters.

"The dress," I repeated.

"The one you're borrowing from Parker's friend," said Rox.

"I saw it last night," Cath cut in, tearing the paper wrapper off a straw. Cath came over because we were working on an American history report together. "It's strapless."

"Sounds sexy," Mita commented.

"And the fabric," Cath elaborated, sticking the straw into a bottle of grapefruit juice. "It's satin, but not the shiny kind. It just sort of . . . glows."

Cath went on describing the dress, and since she was doing such a good job, I only needed to add a word here and there. As we talked, though, I felt less and less like bringing up the food stamps. It was just such a contrast to the fairy-tale ball gown. I shouldn't be embarrassed around my friends, though, I told myself.

I looked around to make sure no one at the nearby tables could hear me. Then I pulled the food stamps out of my book bag and slid them onto the table, keeping them mostly covered with my hand. "Check this out," I said grimly.

Rox, Mita, and Cath peered at the coupon book. "Oh, I remember those," said Rox with a knowing sigh.

Cath looked up at my face, reading me with the

ease of someone who's known me all my life. "You're bummed, huh?"

"Wouldn't you be?" I countered.

"It's not the end of the world," Rox said. "Your mom needs some help right now—anyone would. She'll be back on her feet in no time." Rox put a hand on mine and gave my fingers a squeeze. "Don't worry."

I wanted to cry. "It's kind of embarrassing," I said with a sniffle. "I almost didn't tell you."

"That's crazy," said Mita. "I mean, what are friends for? Richer or poorer, in sickness and in health—"

"That's marriage," I pointed out, tucking the food stamps back into their hiding place.

"Whatever. Tell you what. I'll go shopping with you this afternoon," Mita offered. "I don't have to be at the restaurant until five."

"You're the best," I told her, my eyes shining. "All of you. But don't worry about it, Mita. Daisy will be with me, so I'll manage."

We went back to eating our lunches. I was still dreading the grocery store, but it seemed a little less horrible now that my friends knew about it. They'd put it into perspective for me. Food stamps were just one of those things. Maybe my family didn't have a lot of money, but we were managing.

"Back to the prom," Rox said to me. "Tell Parker if any of his Seagate friends needs a date, I'm free that night."

I cracked a smile. "Will do."

*   *   *

Late that afternoon I picked up Daisy at the junior high after softball practice, then drove slowly back into town. "The speed limit's thirty-five," Daisy pointed out.

I was going about twenty. "Give me a break, okay?" I said. "I just got my license. I don't want to get pulled over."

I couldn't drive much slower than that, though, so eventually we arrived at the Village Market. I parked the station wagon, climbed out slowly, slammed the creaky driver's side door, then took my time locking it even though no one bothers locking a car in the Village Market parking lot. Daisy, meanwhile, had grabbed a shopping cart and was heading into the store.

I trotted after her, shopping list in hand. "Should we split up?" she asked.

"Sure." I scanned the list. "Why don't you grab a couple of loaves of bread and some cereal?" I lowered my voice. "Mom wrote down that the generic cornflakes are on sale."

Daisy strode off, her ponytail swinging purposefully. I wheeled the cart down the produce aisle, grabbing bunches of carrots and bananas and heads of lettuce almost at random. I'd dragged my feet on my way to the store, but now that I was there, I wanted to get this over with as quickly as possible.

In the meat and poultry section I chose value packs of ground beef and chicken. Then I cruised down the dairy aisle, snagging a couple of jugs of milk. Daisy met me near the snack aisle. "How about some cookies?" she suggested.

"They're not on the list," I said, wondering if there was a rule against buying junk food with food stamps. I pictured the checkout clerk frowning at the cookies, then calling the store manager over the loudspeaker. "We should stick to the list," I decided.

"Well, what else do we need?"

I glanced at the list—only one more item. That meant it was about time to head to the checkout counter. I froze, suddenly unable to move my feet. "Rose?" Daisy prompted.

"Um, laundry soap," I told her. "A jumbo box. Whatever's cheapest."

"I'll run and get it. Meet you in line."

"Yeah."

She left me standing near the snack aisle, my heart pounding with dread. *Pull yourself together, Rose Walker*, I thought, wishing I had let Mita come along for moral support. *Have some guts.*

Taking a deep breath, I focused on a boy halfway down the snack aisle. He was of medium height and stocky build and sandy haired, wearing baggy gym shorts, a ripped T-shirt, and a backward Hawk Harbor South Regional H.S. varsity baseball cap. *It's Sully*, I realized, horrified.

My old boyfriend, Brian "Sully" Sullivan, was staring at the shelf in front of him as if choosing between tortilla chips and cheese puffs were the most important decision he'd ever make in his life.

Had he spotted me yet? If he turned his head half an inch, it was all over. He'd grab his bag of chips, then saunter over to say hi. Walk me to the checkout counter . . . and see the food coupons. Sully didn't have a mean bone in his body, and that was the problem—he wouldn't think twice about telling people about the food stamps. It would never occur to him that I would care if people knew. The whole baseball team will know by tomorrow, and their girlfriends. And isn't Sam Conover's sister Kate dating a guy whose cousin goes to Seagate? I thought frantically. What if the word gets back to Parker?

Panic struck like a riptide. Abandoning the shopping cart full of food, I sprinted toward the exit.

Daisy intercepted me. "Rose, where are you going?"

Without answering, I yanked the box of laundry detergent from her hand and stuck it on the nearest shelf. I grabbed her arm, but she resisted me. "We can't leave without the groceries," Daisy said. "Mom'll be mad. If it's about the—*you know*—I'll pay for the stuff. I don't care."

Her selflessness made me feel a thousand times worse, if that were possible. "Just come on," I said, choking back tears.

We drove home in silence—the only sound the humming of the pavement under the wheels. "What are you going to tell Mom?" Daisy asked quietly as I brought the car to a stop on our gravel driveway.

I shrugged. "I'll think of something. Just keep your mouth shut, okay?"

We went into the house. Mom was in the kitchen, sipping a glass of iced tea while she sorted through the day's mail. I wanted to run straight up to my room, but that would only make me look guilty. And I didn't do anything wrong, I told myself.

"Hi, girls," Mom greeted us, looking up with a smile. "Need help carrying in the groceries?"

Daisy was as silent as a stone. "The groceries," I repeated, pretending I didn't know what she was talking about. "Oh, shoot, the groceries! Mom, I'm so sorry. Choral practice ran over, and I was late picking up Daisy, and then I guess I just . . . I'll run back out," I offered, praying she wouldn't call my bluff. "Do you want me to run back out?"

During this Academy Award–winning speech, my mother watched my face steadily. I managed not to turn red, to blink, or to stammer, and I thought I sounded pretty sincere. Maybe too sincere. Could she see through me?

"That's all right, Rose," she said finally. "I can go tomorrow."

We looked at each other a moment. Her face told me that she understood. If she had called me out on my lie, I couldn't possibly have felt worse than I did at that moment. I turned away, sick with guilt and ashamed of myself. "Well, I'm going to start my homework," I told her. "Let me know if you need help with dinner."

"Will do, Rose."

The way she said my name—so full of sympathy and love—made me want to cry.

But as I headed down the hall toward the staircase another emotion began bubbling to the surface: anger. Why should I feel bad about this? I thought. "It's Mom's fault," I muttered under my breath.

Daisy was right behind me on the stairs. "What's Mom's fault?" she wanted to know.

"That we don't have any money," I practically spat out. "Dad would never have let this happen to us. Maybe if Mom had gone to college like everybody else—"

Daisy's blue eyes widened with shock. "Rose!"

"Well, it's true," I said, kicking open the door to my bedroom. "Why should we have to suffer because she can't get her act together?"

Daisy followed me into my room. "Mom's doing her best," she insisted. "I think she's really brave—and resourceful."

My sister's saintly tone made me even madder. "Whose side are you on?" I snapped.

"I'm not on anyone's side," she answered. "I mean, we're all on the same side, aren't we?"

I shook my head, disgusted. "Thanks for the opinion, Miss I-never-do-anything-wrong!" I stomped across the room to my desk. "If you don't *mind*, I have a ton of studying to do."

Daisy stood in the doorway for a few seconds,

biting her lip, her eyebrows furrowed. When I didn't look at her, she finally turned away and disappeared down the hall.

As soon as she was gone the guilt returned. There was no reason to yell at Daisy, I realized. She's just a kid—it's not her fault, either.

Anyway . . . she's right.

With that thought my anger faded, like steam into cold night air. Flopping onto the bed with my Spanish book, I sighed deeply. Who was I really mad at, anyway? It wasn't Daisy's fault we were poor, and it wasn't my fault, and Daisy was right— as good as it felt to blame someone, it wasn't Mom's fault.

I decided that in a little while, I'd hunt up Daisy and apologize. I considered confessing to Mom about chickening out at the Village Market, but I just couldn't. What if she asked me to go back to the store? I wasn't ready for that.

I'm not angry at Mom; I'm angry at the situation. It's nobody's fault, I reasoned as I worked through my Spanish assignment. Nobody's fault, nobody's fault.

Shoving my book aside, I dropped my head onto the pillow and let out another deep sigh. Maybe it was nobody's fault, but it was still horrible.

Five

The South Regional junior prom was taking place the same night as the Seagate Academy prom, though it would be held in the school gym, not at a fancy country club. Cath was going with Tony, a guy she'd just started dating, and Mita and Rox were both planning to go to a big sophomore class bash at the beach. We decided to get together at Cath's on Saturday morning for a pre-prom-and-party manicure session.

We set up in Cath's bedroom. She is seriously into being a Beautiful Person and could practically open her own salon—she has a vanity table cluttered with dozens of kinds and colors of makeup, all sorts of hairbrushes and curlers, and enough cotton balls to decorate a parade float. She took turns giving me, Rox, and Mita manicures. Then Rox did Cath's nails while Mita helped me experiment with hairstyles.

"I wish we were all going to the same party tonight," Rox said as she dipped the nail brush into a bottle of polish and went to work on Cath's left thumb.

"Tony and I will come by the beach later if the dance gets boring," Cath promised.

"Where's he taking you for dinner before-hand?" Mita asked.

"Leonardo's." Cath rolled her eyes. "Italian, of course."

"You'll get spaghetti sauce on your prom dress," I predicted with a grin.

"Give me a little credit!" she said, laughing. "I won't order marinara."

"How about you?" Mita asked as she twisted my hair into a French knot. "Think you'll be able to drag *Parker*"—at his name, she batted her dark eyes playfully—"to the beach when the Seagate prom winds down?"

Parker's not really the type to party on the beach in a tuxedo. "We'll see," I said. "I think one of his friends is having an after-party. He'll probably want to stick with the Seagate crowd."

"So, guess who called me last night," Rox said, her blue eyes sparkling. She placed the nail polish bottle on the vanity to free up her hands for a dramatic gesture. "Kurt Blessing."

"Oooh!" We gave an appropriately enthusiastic group squeal—Kurt Blessing is one of the cutest boys in our class.

"Why on *earth* did he call you?" Mita teased. Guys are always calling Rox—she has big blue eyes, tons of wavy strawberry blond hair, and a killer figure, not to mention a great personality.

"He wanted to be sure I was going to the party tonight," Rox replied.

"Oooh!" we chorused again.

"So what you're saying," Cath said, "is that by the time Tony and I show up, you and Kurt will have disappeared into the dunes for your own private—"

Rox slapped the back of Cath's still drying hand. "Dirty mind."

"What do you think about your hair?" Mita asked me. "Do you like it? Or is it too formal?" She answered her own question before I had a chance. "Maybe you should wear it down. What if you brushed it back like this and then tucked this part and clipped this part and . . ."

I sat quietly while Mita fussed. Rox and Cath were still joking about Kurt. Suddenly I felt a pang. They're going to have so much fun tonight, I thought, feeling left out. I wish I were going to the beach party, too.

Then I caught myself. I was going to the prom with Parker Kemp. Nothing could be more fun than that. Right?

"Your hair looks so pretty," Lily chirped that evening.

I was standing in front of my dresser and mirror in my underwear and stockings, getting ready for the dance. Lily had been driving me nuts peeking into my room, so I'd finally invited her in to watch me put on my makeup and get dressed.

I'd decided on a French twist. It was a more formal style than I usually liked, but I wanted to look sophisticated. I stuck a bobby pin into my hair, capturing a stray wisp. "Do you really think so?" I asked anxiously. Ordinarily my eight-year-old sister wouldn't be my first choice as a fashion consultant, but her opinion was better than nothing. And suddenly, for some reason, I was nervous. About my appearance . . . about everything. Will I look right? Will I act right? What if Parker ends up wishing he'd taken someone else to the dance?

"I really think so," Lily declared.

"Well, then, how about my makeup? Did I put on too much eye shadow?" I blinked, then patted my cheeks. "I'm not tan yet. Should I wear blush?"

"You look fine the way you are," Lily said.

"Fine?"

"I mean, *great*," she corrected herself.

With a wry laugh I reached for my jewelry box. I fastened the silver necklace Parker had given me around my neck and then went to the closet, where Valerie's dress waited for me.

I took the dress from the dry cleaner's bag. I laid it out on the bed and for a moment just looked at it admiringly. Then I unzipped the zipper down the back, careful not to snag the delicate fabric, and prepared to step into the dress.

Ten seconds passed, then thirty. I stood holding the dress for a full minute. "What's wrong?" Lily wanted to know.

I stared at the dress in my hands. What *was* wrong? I wasn't a hundred percent sure, but I knew one thing for certain. "I can't wear this dress," I said quietly.

"Why not?" Lily asked. "It's really pretty."

I bit my lip. Was it because it belonged to someone else, a girl I didn't know very well? I recalled my joking remark to Cath about getting spaghetti sauce on her dress. "I won't be able to relax—I'll be too worried that I'll spill something on it," I said to Lily. "Or rip it or something."

Lily seemed satisfied with that explanation, and I was, too. But was it the real reason? I found myself thinking about my conversation with Parker the day I'd shown him the dress from Second Time Around. I'd been so excited about it, but he'd dismissed it with a glance.

Why did it even matter to him what dress I wore?

"I'm going to wear the other dress," I decided suddenly, sticking Valerie's dress back in the dry cleaner's bag before I could change my mind.

I slipped into the sage green dress and immediately knew I was doing the right thing. It felt soft, silky, comfortable. I didn't look like a supermodel, but I looked pretty. I looked like me.

Lily squinted at me. "Now the necklace looks wrong," she pointed out.

Of course Lily, the costume jewelry queen, was right. I returned Parker's necklace to my jewelry box, putting on the one my mother had given me. The tiny gold rosebud on the delicate chain was perfect with the old-fashioned dress. "There," I said. "I'm ready."

Lily clapped, her eyes shining. "Parker will think you're so beautiful!"

The tiniest of doubts flickered in my heart. I ignored it. He's taking *me* to the dance, not the dress, I reminded myself. "I hope so," I replied.

"Daisy, don't talk to Parker about sports, okay? He's not into baseball or any of that stuff. Lily, couldn't you wear something normal for once in your life? And Toad, if Henry or any other rodent comes within fifty feet of this house tonight, you're doomed. Got that?"

It was seven o'clock—Parker would be ringing the doorbell any minute now. Meanwhile, seeing me off on my first prom date had turned into a Walker Family Event. My three sisters were lurking in the front hall. Daisy had an old Polaroid camera, and Lily was clutching the box with Parker's boutonniere. Laurel was without pets— that I could see, anyway—but as usual she carried the faintest whiff of eau de barnyard.

"If I can't talk to him about sports, what should I talk about?" Daisy asked.

"You don't have to talk about *anything*," I said, grabbing a bottle of room spray from the powder room and giving Laurel a quick spritz. "Just, you know, smile." I took Daisy's baseball cap off her head and tossed it in the coat closet. "Say hello and then vamoose."

The doorbell rang. We all jumped. "It's him!" Lily squealed excitedly.

"I'll open it," Laurel offered.

"No, I will," said Lily. A shoving match ensued. I elbowed past them to open it myself.

Parker stepped into the hall, a white florist's box in his hand. He looked incredibly handsome in his black tuxedo and cummerbund. "Hi," I said breathlessly. "You look great!"

I waited for my kiss. Instead Parker gave me an up-and-down look. "What happened to Val's dress?" he asked.

That threw me off balance for a minute. What happened to "Hi, Rose, you look wonderful"? I thought. "I, uh . . . the zipper was broken," I fibbed, blushing. I darted a don't-you-dare-speak glance at Lily. "I just noticed when I went to put it on tonight. Don't worry," I babbled on, "I'll get it fixed before I give it back to Valerie. I'll—"

"It's too bad because . . ." Parker shook his head, then gave me a quick peck on the cheek. "Never mind. You look fine. And hey. What have we here?" he asked in a patronizing tone. "Dorothy from *The Wizard of Oz*?"

This is the moment to point out that Lily had curled her long hair into ringlets and was wearing an old-fashioned blue pinafore with a white blouse and button-up shoes. "*Alice in Wonderland*," she told him, frowning a little at his mistake.

"Right. You're the one who likes to dress up." Parker turned to Laurel. "And you're in, what, third grade?"

Laurel's eyebrows drew together. "Fifth," she said from her hiding place behind Daisy.

"And you'll be starting high school next year, right?" Parker said to Daisy. "Breaking a lot of hearts, too."

"I *hope* not," Daisy replied, making a disgusted face.

I'd been holding my breath, waiting for one of my siblings to do something humiliating. Henry the mouse hadn't made an appearance, though, so maybe this was my lucky night.

Done with small talk, Parker turned his back on my sisters. I saw them exchange meaningful glances. "Let's get this show on the road," he said to me.

"No, wait." Daisy whipped out the camera. "We need a picture!"

Just then Mom showed up. She'd been at the dining room table, paying some bills. "Let's take a whole bunch," she suggested. "Rose, why don't you give Parker his boutonniere?"

Daisy snapped photos of Parker pinning the corsage to my dress and me pinning the boutonniere to his jacket. Then we posed for about twenty pictures standing with our arms around each other. I felt like an idiot.

Finally Parker said, "We really need to get going, Rose." He put a hand on the small of my back and practically shoved me out the door.

"Bye!" I called back to my family.

"Have fun!" Mom said.

"Wow," I couldn't help saying when we entered the lobby of Rocky Point Country Club.

It was like a movie set: chandeliers and gilded mirrors, oriental rugs and ornate furniture, glass cabinets filled with silver trophies, and photographs of yachts on all the walls. "Haven't you ever been here?" Parker asked, one eyebrow lifted slightly.

Until I'd met Parker, I hadn't even known anyone who was a member. "Um, it's been a couple of years," I lied. "I'd forgotten how pretty it is."

The prom was being held in a ballroom that opened onto a stone terrace. There was a view of the moonlit golf course in one direction and of the marina in the other. We had eaten dinner at the Harborside before heading over to the country club, so the dance was already in full swing. As soon as Parker and I appeared we were surrounded by his friends. I spotted Valerie's brother, Stephen, standing at a distance. "Who did he come with?" I asked Parker.

Parker shrugged. "Mathias? He's probably stag. No one's good enough for that guy."

Parker, David, Chip, and the other guys went through the usual routine of high fives and pounding one another on the back. Meanwhile the Seagate girls descended on me.

"Rose, what a sweet dress," exclaimed Tiffany Greer, who goes out with Parker's friend David. "Did you make it yourself?"

"Um," I began.

"I love it," gushed Caitlin O'Connor. "It's like *The Age of Innocence* or something. The Victorian look really looks good on her, don't you think, Amanda?"

"She's braver than me," Amanda Morrow agreed. "I have to go with the trends, you know?"

I'd never heard such backhanded compliments in my life. I should have laughed out loud. Instead I cringed, hoping Parker wasn't listening.

Valerie Mathias strolled by with her date. She was wearing a very short, sexy, black off-the-shoulder dress. She paused just long enough to note, "The blue-and-white dress didn't work out, huh?"

"Uh—no," I replied lamely.

"Too bad." As she drifted off she lowered her voice, speaking to her date, but I heard her clearly. "I can see why she wanted to borrow something from me."

I decided not to let it bother me. What do I care if the Seagate girls are snobs? I thought. That's not exactly news.

The band was great and I was dying to dance, but Parker wanted to stand around and gab with his friends. I tried to take part in the conversation, but it was hard—there were too many inside jokes. Every now and then someone would clue me in, but instead of making me feel included, it only made it more apparent that I was an outsider. Then they all started comparing their plans for the summer. Aspen, Europe, sailing, tennis. Nobody mentioned a job.

"Let's dance, Parker," I said impulsively.

We danced to a few songs, and I started to relax. It felt good to be in Parker's arms. Then in between songs Valerie appeared. "You don't mind if I borrow your date, do you?" she asked with a sly smile, hooking her arm through Parker's.

What could I say? I'd borrowed her dress, even if I didn't end up wearing it. And Parker didn't look as if he thought having to dance with Valerie was too much of a burden. "Sure," I replied. "Go ahead."

I wandered over to the food. As I poured myself a cup of punch and turned to watch the dancers, I wondered why I was experiencing a feeling of déjà vu. When Stephen Mathias walked up to me, I figured it out. It was just like at my surprise party.

"Would you like to dance?" he asked politely.

I blushed, feeling somewhat idiotic. "We don't have to," I told him. "I mean—"

"I'd like to." Stephen stuck out an elbow so I had to take his arm. "Just a couple of songs."

Just my luck, right then the band started playing a slow song. Stephen took my right hand in his left and placed his left hand on my waist. I just kind of shuffled, but he was doing something fancy with his feet. "You really know how to dance," I observed.

"Ballroom lessons when I was in sixth grade," he told me.

"You're kidding!"

"My mother made me take them. But it comes in handy now and then," he said. "At debutante parties and stuff."

"Oh," I said.

For some reason I found myself blushing again.

Stephen's hand was very warm on my waist. "This is a pretty dress," he remarked.

I glanced up at him. "You're joking, right?"

"Of course not. I like it."

"Then you're the only one."

He was still looking into my eyes. "They're just jealous," he said.

"Who?" I asked, wondering if he'd overheard my conversation with Amanda, Tiffany, and Caitlin.

"Because you don't feel like you have to look like every other girl here," he went on. "You have your own style."

I realized that Stephen was right. The Seagate girls had made me feel like the poor relation—I'd almost forgotten that I'd *chosen* to wear this dress. "Thanks," I said softly.

When the song ended, I stepped away from Stephen. "I should go find Parker," I told him, hunting for my boyfriend in the crowded room. "He's probably looking for me."

A funny expression crossed Stephen's face. "I don't see him," he said. He took my hand again. "One more song, okay?"

"Well, okay," I agreed.

We danced one more song, and then I went to the ladies' room. When I came out, I still didn't see Parker, but I did see Amanda. "Three girls have the exact same dress as me," she moaned, sucking in her thin cheeks in irritation. "Can you believe it? And I went all the way to Boston for it just so this wouldn't happen!"

You should have shopped at Second Time Around, I thought smugly. "Bad luck," I said.

"So, I saw you dancing with Stephen Mathias," Amanda said. "That's kind of an honor, you know."

I didn't know. "What do you mean?"

"He used to go out with this Seagate girl two classes ahead of him," Amanda explained as she fiddled with her corsage, which had come unpinned. "Camilla Larson. They broke up right after she left for college last fall, though, so he's available, but I guess none of us meets his high standards or something. He hasn't asked anyone else out this whole year. There." She patted her corsage, then gave me a distracted smile. "See you, Rose."

Amanda melted into the crowd. A minute later I saw her dancing with her date. I glimpsed Stephen, too, standing with a group of guys whom I guessed were juniors and seniors. I studied him thoughtfully. So, he didn't have a date, and he didn't seem to be dancing much, but he had danced with me. How come? Did he feel sorry for me? I hoped not.

I made a tour of the ballroom and finally spotted Parker and Valerie. A song had just ended, but they were still standing close together. Before drawing apart, Valerie whispered something in Parker's ear that made him grin. Parker whispered something back, gave her a little hug around the waist, and then headed in my direction.

He gave me the same kind of hug he'd given Valerie. I tried hard not to notice or care. "Having fun?" he asked.

Was I having fun standing by myself, dodging insults about my dress, and watching Parker dance with someone else? I smiled at him brightly and gave Parker the only answer I knew he would accept. "Sure!"

Knowing it was a special night for me, Mom had relaxed my usual curfew, so Parker and I went to a couple of after-parties and I didn't get home until nearly four in the morning. After we kissed good night, Parker drove off as quietly as he could, the Jeep's tires crunching on the gravel driveway, and I tiptoed into the dark and silent house.

In my room I left the light off, but the moon was shining into my window, so I could still see myself as I stood in front of the mirror over my dresser. For a long moment I stared at my shadowy reflection. I didn't look like a girl who'd just been to her first prom with the boy of her dreams. I looked like I was about to cry—which I was.

Disappointment washed over me. Thinking back on the evening, I couldn't find fault with Parker. He'd been the perfect date as always. Sure, he'd danced a few times with other girls, but that seemed to be the Seagate style. His good night kisses had been passionate. He'd told me, not for the first time, that he was crazy about my long blond hair, my big blue eyes, my smooth skin. Shouldn't that make me happy?

Tears welled up in my eyes and spilled down my cheeks. I ripped the drooping corsage from my dress and threw it on the floor. The gold rosebud and chain around my neck glimmered softly in the moonlight—I yanked it off, too, then shoved the necklace to the back of my dresser drawer, thinking unreasonably, I hate this tacky rosebud charm! I hate it! I'll never wear it again.

Quickly unzipping my dress, I wriggled free of it as fast as I could. I crumpled the soft fabric in my hands and tossed it into the corner, giving it a kick for good measure.

I'd been trying to blink back my tears, but now they were flowing. I grabbed a nightgown from my dresser drawer and pulled it over my head, noticing that it was on backward and inside out but not caring. I crawled into bed and buried my face in my pillow to stifle my sobs. Outside my window the sky was gray with light as I finally cried myself to sleep.

Six

"Don't you just love summer?" Rox asked me a week and a half later.

It was midmorning on a Tuesday, and we were strolling along the sidewalk in downtown Hawk Harbor, enjoying the still fresh freedom of summer vacation. The sun was shining, and there was a warm sea breeze. Main Street still wasn't too busy—things wouldn't really pick up until Fourth of July weekend—but most of the shops and restaurants were open, and the town had a clean, just-washed look. I pushed my sunglasses up on the bridge of my nose and tipped my head back a bit, shaking out my loose hair. "I love summer, generally speaking," I admitted. "But *this* summer . . ."

"Are you still moping because you can't go to Wildwood?" Rox wanted to know.

I shrugged. Just the day before I'd gotten a letter from Julianne Greenberg. Camp had only just started, but she already had ten hilarious wish-you-were-here stories. The worst of it was she didn't know the real reason I'd turned down the counselor job, so she assumed I was having a great time, too. When I'd told her the news, I'd whitewashed the situation, throwing in a lie about a family trip. "Have I really been moping?" I asked Rox.

"Maybe not *moping*," she said, "but I could tell you've been bummed."

"I was at first," I agreed, "but I'm trying not to act like a baby about it. I mean, a lot of things had to change with Dad . . . gone." It was still hard for me to say *dead*. It sounded so final.

We were silent for a moment. "But there's a silver lining," Rox pointed out. "Since you're staying in Hawk Harbor, you'll get to see more of Parker."

"Right," I said. I couldn't admit, though, that ever since prom night, thinking about Parker made me so insecure that I felt nauseated. I hated feeling that way. Everyone assumed I'd had a great time at the Seagate prom, and I hadn't disillusioned them. Lying was getting easier for me. "He and his dad have this big just-us-guys sailing trip planned for most of August, but yeah. 'A silver lining.'" I had to laugh. "I sound like Daisy. That's the kind of sappy thing she'd say."

"Hey, it beats the alternative," Rox said. She stopped, gesturing at a storefront. "What do you say we try here first?"

Rox's words reminded me of why we'd come into town in the first place—we were job hunting. Our other friends already had jobs for the summer: Cath would be pitching in at her family's hardware store while Mita would help at her parents' restaurant.

Suppressing a sigh, I peered into the window of Cecilia's. "It doesn't look half bad," I said. And there was a Help Wanted sign in the window. "Okay." I straightened my shoulders. "Let's get this over with."

An hour later we concluded our parade of Main Street with a stop at Patsy's Diner. Rox didn't even have to fill out an application—Patsy hired her on the spot. "I can't believe it was that easy!" Rox exclaimed as we emerged into the sunshine. "Patsy said if I do a good job busing tables, she'll promote me to waitress after just a couple of weeks. Then I'll really be making decent money with tips and all."

I high-fived Rox, meanwhile biting my tongue. Maybe waitresses make good money, but you wouldn't catch me dishing out french fries and tuna melts in a tacky beige uniform. I gave a silent shudder at the thought of what Parker would say.

I'd applied for three jobs. "I hope I get the position at Cecilia's," I confided. "Mrs. King said she'd let me know tomorrow after she interviews a few more people."

Rox hooked her arm through mine. "We'll be working girls," she said cheerfully. "It'll be fun."

Working girls. I tried to look at it the way Rox did, with a positive attitude—the ol' silver lining approach. I'm not going to Wildwood because I'm not a kid anymore. No camp and no hanging out at the beach, either. I'll be working nine to five, five days a week. But I'll be making money, my own money. My expression brightened somewhat. "Maybe I'll even get an employee's discount!"

*   *   *

"The hours are pretty flexible," I told Parker two days later. "I won't have to work every weekend. And Mrs. King seems really nice. I mean, like she'll be a cool boss even though she's pretty old, forty-five or so."

Parker had invited me over, and we were hanging out by the pool in his backyard. I was wearing a navy-and-white flowered bikini—last year's, but it still looked good on me.

Parker's house is one of the most beautiful in Hawk Harbor. It's right on the water, three stories high, with a widow's walk and painted white with black shutters. It was what our house might look like if we poured a million dollars into fixing it up. Not that I was envious—well, maybe a little. The Kemps have servants, too, an older couple named Mr. and Mrs. Birtwhistle, who live in an apartment over the four-car garage.

Mr. and Mrs. Birtwhistle do everything—shop, cook, clean, garden, you name it. Which means Mrs. Kemp doesn't have to lift a finger around the house, and she doesn't have a job, so she has plenty of time to sit by the pool, and that's what she was doing right then, just like Parker and me. She was on the opposite side of the pool, though, in a black strapless bathing suit, her eyes hidden behind big Jackie O. sunglasses. She is very blond and very thin and very tan. She kept her nose in a glossy travel magazine, putting it down now and then to make a call on the cordless phone. She didn't speak to me or Parker.

I was still waiting for him to say something about my summer job. "Congratulations" or "Nice going" or something. Finally he grunted, "It's too bad you'll be working. We could have a lot of fun out on the boat."

"I won't be working all the time," I reminded him.

"So you'll be what, a salesgirl?"

On the surface it was an innocent question, but Parker managed to make *salesgirl* sound like *prostitute* or something. My cheeks burned. "Yeah, I'll be a salesgirl," I said in a defensive tone. "It's a nice store."

Parker laughed. "For Hawk Harbor. Hey, I'm roasting. Let's get wet."

Parker grabbed my hand and pulled me toward the pool. We dove into the cool water and started splashing around. I dunked Parker. He grabbed me around the waist and kissed me on the lips.

We were soaking wet and nearly naked, and the kiss made me kind of uncomfortable. I shot a glance at Mrs. Kemp, but she clearly couldn't care less what we did.

Parker gave me another kiss, and I tried to enjoy it. I tried not to think about him hating my dress and dancing with Valerie at the prom, about my summer job, about my family, about food stamps.

For just half an hour I wanted my life to be simple and perfect—for it to be nothing more than me and Parker in a turquoise blue swimming pool on a sunny summer day.

"Darn," my mother exclaimed.

I was setting the dining room table when I

heard a saucepan clatter on the stove, its contents sizzling angrily. I looked into the kitchen at Mom—she'd dropped the wooden spoon and was shaking her right hand in the air. "Are you all right, Mom?" I asked.

She nodded, brushing the hair back from her face with an impatient gesture. "Just clumsy, that's all," she said. "Dinner's ready, Rose. Would you call your sisters?"

I shouted up the stairs and out the back door, and in a few minutes Daisy and Lily showed up. The four of us sat down to supper. "Where's Laurel?" I asked as Mom served the food.

"You remember Jack, who found the raccoons?" she replied, scooping mashed potatoes onto Lily's plate. "Cute kid, very well behaved. He invited her over for dinner."

I was kind of surprised Laurel went. I didn't really expect her to make friends with a boy. "That's great," I said.

"It's too bad she's not here, though," said Mom, "because I wanted to have a family meeting."

Oh no, not again, I thought. "What's up?" I asked warily.

"We just need to talk about chores," she said. "There's a lot of work that has to be done around the house and yard, and we need to do it ourselves. And I could use some help with the housework now that I'm working."

Against my will, I pictured the Kemps' spotless house, with Mrs. Birtwhistle busy in the kitchen and Mr. Birtwhistle busy in the yard. "Sure, Mom," Daisy said. "When Laurel comes home, you can just tell us what we should do."

We all started eating. "Great chicken, Mom," Daisy declared.

We'd been having chicken practically every night. It was always chicken or spaghetti, or at least that's how it seemed. Chicken with rice, chicken with pasta, chicken pot pie, chicken soup. "Thanks, sweetheart," she said. She looked very tired.

Susie Sunshine tried again. "How was work today, Mom?"

"Okay. They're giving me more hours starting next week—thirty-five up from twenty-five. Almost but not quite full-time."

"That's great!" I exclaimed, envisioning an end to our money problems.

Mom sighed, and my spirits sank again. "It's still not enough. Even if I were working forty hours a week with full benefits, I don't think I could make ends meet. Not at this job."

"Well, here," said Daisy brightly. She pulled something from the pocket of her shorts and placed it on the table. It was a wad of dollar bills. "Chores are one thing, but I want to do more. I've been saving my baby-sitting money. It's not tons, but now that it's summer, I'll really start raking it in. I've lined up two steady baby-sitting jobs, plus I put up flyers all over town about doing yard work."

Lily glanced from Daisy to Mom, her face

solemn. "Mommy, should I try to make some money, too?" she asked.

"Of course not, honey," Mom said. She turned to Daisy, her eyes watery. "I can't take your baby-sitting money, Daisy. There are lots of things you need for yourself."

"I'm going to make more," Daisy insisted. She shoved the bills toward Mom. "Really, Mom. You have to let me help." Daisy's eyes looked misty now, too. "I want to help."

I ate my chicken in silence, my own eyes prickling with unexpected tears.

I thought again about Parker's "perfect" life. I'd rather be rich than poor—who wouldn't? To live in a house like Parker's, with my own pool, my own car, servants. But then I thought about Parker's mother, the elegant, stylish, ice-cold, disinterested Mrs. Kemp, and my heart ached with love for my own mother and sisters. Maybe we had to work hard, but didn't that bring us closer in the end?

Honestly, Rose, I asked myself. Would you trade your life if you could?

Seven

The summer days sped by, and I fell into a routine that wasn't half bad. I had thought I would hate getting up early every single morning—I thought I'd hate work, period. To my surprise, though, I liked working at the boutique. After a week I stopped moping about Wildwood. Rox made more money than I did, but at the end of the day she had to shampoo her hair for half an hour to get out the french fry smell. No, thanks!

So, my job was fine. Days off were still the best, though. Today Parker was taking me sailing for the first time.

We met at the marina. Parker's family's yacht, *Kiss and Tell*, was moored at slip nine, and Parker was already there, kneeling on the wooden deck with a rag in his hand.

"What are you doing?" I asked, swinging myself onto the boat.

"Just a little touch-up," he answered. He screwed the top back on a jar of wax. "There's always some little project, you know?"

"Yeah," I said, intrigued by the fact that Parker didn't mind working—when it came to the boat.

I popped a CD—No Doubt—into the boom box while we motored into the harbor. "When will you put up the sails?" I asked Parker.

"As soon as we get beyond that buoy." He pointed to the channel marker. "Man, those fishing boats stink. There should be a law."

Two lobster boats passed us, heading in the opposite direction. I knew both the fishermen—one was Nathan Beale, Rox's dad. A year ago one of those stinking boats might have been my father's. Which of course Parker didn't know because I'd never told him.

I looked at Parker, about to tell him off. Those are real boats and real people, trying to make an honest living. How dare you? But the words died on my lips.

Parker was smiling fondly at me. "Did I ever tell you I love the way you look on this boat?"

For once I wasn't pleased by the compliment. "I'm just here for decoration?" I asked somewhat testily.

His left hand on the wheel, Parker reached for me with the other, laughing. "Yeah, and if you're not available, I'll call up some other gorgeous, bikini-clad blond," he teased.

Parker nuzzled my neck. I stiffened. "Is that a threat?" I asked him.

He sat back. "Is what a threat?"

"When I'm not around, you—"

"Hey, you know I don't like to sail by myself. There's always someone else along or usually a bunch of people. If you didn't work so much, you wouldn't miss out. Which isn't to say you're not the one I want to be with. Let's mellow out, okay?"

Parker faced forward again, steering past a buoy. The breeze was picking up, so I took over the helm while he put up the sails. For a few minutes we were too busy to talk, which gave me time to think. *Why is it always "I love the way you look"?* I wondered. *And that crack about the fishing boats. He wouldn't have said it if he knew about my dad, but still . . . There's a lot he doesn't know about me,* I realized a little sadly. *We'd been going out for three months. Why were we still practically strangers?*

The next morning I made a couple of sales as soon as Cecilia's opened. Then during a quiet spell I dusted shelves and unpacked some new inventory— leather belts and other accessories. Mrs. King was letting me experiment with different ways of arranging things, so I decided to loop the belts over a piece of driftwood in the front window, alternating them with knotted silk scarves.

I was working on my display when the little bell over the door jingled. Straightening up, I pushed back my hair and prepared to smile winningly at my customer. Then I saw who it was, and my mouth just dropped open.

Stephen was wearing the standard Rocky Point uniform: khaki shorts, a weathered designer polo, boat shoes without socks, sunglasses. His glossy dark hair flopped down on his forehead. "Hi, Rose," he said.

"Hi," I replied.

I returned to the scarves and belts, ducking my head to hide my face behind my hair. He must've walked into the wrong store, I thought, hoping he'd be gone when I looked up again.

He wasn't. I remembered my position as a helpful salesclerk. "Um, is there something I can help you with?" I asked.

Stephen leaned against the counter. "I like your display," he remarked. "You're artistic."

I turned red. Did I detect a note of sarcasm? I couldn't tell. "Um, thanks," I mumbled.

"So, yeah, there is," he went on.

"There is what?" I asked, mad at myself for letting him throw me off balance but unable to keep from blushing more.

"There is something you can help me with. If you would," he added politely. He spread his hands and raised his eyebrows in an expression of cluelessness. "My grandmother's seventy-fifth birthday. What should I give her?"

"Hmmm. It depends," I replied. "Is she an old old lady or a kind of hip old lady? We have these paperweights with shells inside the glass. They're pretty. Then we have these scarves—flashier. Or how about a pair of sunglasses?"

"I gave her a Dave Matthews Band CD for her last birthday," Stephen told me.

I grinned. "Let's pick out some shades."

I expected him to take his gift-wrapped package and jet. Instead he hung out a while longer. "Don't you have to get back to work?" I asked, even though judging by his killer tan, he didn't have a summer job.

"I've got half an hour until my next lesson," he answered, explaining, "I teach soccer."

"You do?" I asked.

"Yeah," he said. "To a bunch of eighth graders." He smiled and added, "They're a handful."

"I bet," I said.

He fiddled with one of the scarves on the rack by the register. "So—what's Parker up to today?"

"Sailing, of course," I replied.

"Who with?"

I shrugged. "Some of his Rocky Point friends, probably. Or maybe your sister and that gang." I tipped my head to one side, wondering why Stephen was interested. "He doesn't always give me a detailed report."

He looked uncomfortable, as if he wanted to say more, but he just shrugged. "Well, hey," he said. "I'll see you around."

I nodded. "Right."

"Thanks again for helping me pick out a gift."

"That's what they pay me for."

He was still standing there, his eyes on my face. Once again I felt a flush creep up my neck to my cheeks. "So long," he said, finally turning toward the door.

"Bye," I said.

*　　*　　*

"So, what does everyone feel like doing?" Parker asked.

It was Saturday evening, and a bunch of people were flopped on chairs around the swimming pool in Parker's backyard, munching chips and salsa and watching the sun set. We'd spent the afternoon playing round-robin tennis at the country club, and everyone was beat. Beat and bored—at least I was. I'm not much of a tennis player and couldn't see the point, frankly, of playing game after game after game, but I'd gone along with it. If I'd sat out, Parker would've chosen another partner—maybe Valerie, who unfortunately was part of the group, as was her brother, Stephen. My impression was that Stephen didn't hang out with Parker and Valerie a whole lot, but he'd brought along some of his own friends for tennis, who were cool. Stephen had won more games than anyone, even Parker.

"There's a new Italian restaurant in Kent," Valerie said, snapping a tortilla chip in two and carefully eating half of it. "How about going out for dinner and then seeing a movie?"

"We could just stay here," Chip suggested, stretching his arms over his head and yawning widely. "Get takeout and delve into Kemp's video collection."

"Fine with me," David said.

"Oh, come on," wheedled Valerie. She crossed her slim, tanned legs. She was wearing a very short white tennis dress that managed to be prim and sexy at the same time. "Don't be such a slug. Who's up for trying La Trattoria?"

I stifled a yawn of my own. Another night sitting around a table in a stuffy, overpriced restaurant, I thought. I looked at Parker, who was looking at Valerie. I could tell he was about to vote for La Trattoria. "I've got an idea," I burst out.

"You do?" said Parker, sounding surprised. Usually when we're with his friends, I just go along with whatever he wants to do.

"Have any of you guys ever been to the Rusty Nail?" I asked. "I think some friends of mine might show up there tonight. Why don't we all go?"

"Isn't that the dive on Old Boston Post Road?" Chip asked. "I mean, it's just townies, isn't it? I mean—" He broke off, apparently realizing for the first time who he was talking to, his face red under his tan.

"Don't knock it if you haven't tried it," I said lightly, although my blood was boiling. "It may not look like much from the street, but they have pool tables and video games, and on Saturday night there's a deejay who plays great dance music. It's a lot of fun," I promised, turning to Parker.

I waited for him to render a verdict—we were all waiting. But Stephen was the one who spoke up first. "I read something in the paper about the Rusty Nail," he said. "It sounds like it rocks. Let's do something new."

Parker shrugged carelessly. "Sure. I'm up for it."

"Cool," I said, flashing Stephen a grateful look.

Out of the corner of my eye I saw Valerie purse her lips—she looked as if she'd just bitten into a lemon. I smothered a triumphant grin.

Chip was partly right—the Rusty Nail *is* kind of a dive. There's no interior decoration to speak of: bare wood walls and floors, exposed beams in the ceiling, no-nonsense tables and chairs. But it's the only place anywhere near Hawk Harbor with live music that lets in kids under eighteen, and because it looks like somebody's unfinished basement, you really feel like you can let loose and have a good time. And that's just what my friends and I like to do.

I spotted Rox, Cath, and Mita along with a mob of other people I knew, and we spent a few minutes greeting one another noisily. Parker stayed with me, but he didn't say much, just smiled politely at everyone. Right away it was obvious that he and the prep school/summer house crowd were fish out of water. A couple of them at least made a good-faith effort to unbend a little and have fun— Stephen grabbed a cue and challenged Cath's boyfriend, Tony, to a friendly game of pool, and Amanda accepted Sully's invitation to dance. But the rest of Parker's cronies stayed on the fringes, not even bothering to hide their disdain.

Parker's reaction was hard to read. For some reason I really wanted us to have a good time, and I wanted us to have it at the Rusty Nail—on my turf, among my friends. I realized in a flash that I wanted Parker to prove something to me: to prove that he really did love me. Me, Rose Annabelle Walker, a local girl.

He hadn't spoken since we entered the Rusty Nail except to say a polite hello to my friends. Now I turned to him and took his hand, leaning close so I wouldn't have to shout. "Want to dance?"

"Actually I was just wondering how long we needed to stick around here," he said.

I wrinkled my forehead. "I thought you were up for trying something new."

"No offense," Parker said. "But is this really your kind of place?"

"My friends and I come here all the time," I told him.

"Okay. Forget I said that." He slipped an arm around my waist. "You want to dance? We'll dance."

I gave Parker a thank-you kiss. For a minute or two after we started dancing, I thought everything was going to be okay. Parker seemed to be loosening up, and when the song ended, he actually gave me a smile.

Just then the deejay made an announcement. "Saturday is open mike night," he bellowed into the microphone. There was a lot of clapping and whistling. "Who's got a guitar? A harmonica? A few good jokes?"

"Oh, man," Parker said. "I can't wait to hear what this crowd does for open mike night."

I flinched a little at that but made no comment.

Maybe he didn't mean anything by it. After all, the crowd *was* a little rowdy.

"I'm heading to the bar for some soda," Parker said. "Want anything?"

I asked for a Coke and made my way over to Mita, Cath, and Rox.

"Hey, Sully, get up there and flex your muscles," Tony yelled. Everybody but Parker's posse burst out laughing.

Sully yelled something back, his language slightly off-color, to put it politely, and we laughed harder. Then this guy who'd just graduated, Jeremy Pratt, swaggered up with his electric guitar. He plugged into an amp and deafened us with a screeching guitar solo that we all bopped to wildly even though he couldn't carry a tune for his life. Then another guy told a bunch of really stupid jokes, which we laughed at because sometimes when you're in the right mood, anything's funny.

A guy moved up next to me. Assuming it was Parker, I put a hand on his arm. Stephen looked down at me and I pulled my hand back quickly, blushing at my mistake. "I wish I had the guts to get up there," he said.

"Go on, do it!" Cath urged.

He shook his head, smiling kind of shyly. "I'm not that good."

"All it takes is enthusiasm," Rox said.

"What have you got to lose?" Mita agreed. "You couldn't be worse than what we've already seen."

Stephen didn't budge, though, so they started working on me.

"Come on, Rose," Cath coaxed. "Get up there and sing."

"No way," I said, although I was secretly tempted.

Parker reappeared and put an arm firmly around my waist just as Mita shouted, "She's got a great voice!"

"Yeah, Rose, sing something!" Sully bellowed helpfully.

The crowd started to chant my name. I looked up at Parker for encouragement. He rolled his eyes.

"Rose doesn't want to sing," Parker announced loudly.

"Whoa, hold on." My eyes widened in surprise. "How do you know what I—"

"Let's go, okay, Rose?" Parker cut in.

His arm was still around me, but I pulled away from him before he could propel me toward the exit. "I don't *want* to leave, Parker," I said.

"You're not going to sing, though, are you?" He was pleading with me.

We stared at each other, and for a second I hesitated.

I wanted Parker to love me and be proud of me. But I had to wonder why it mattered so much what I wore and what I did. Besides, I love to sing. That was one of the many things Parker didn't know about me. It's time for him to see the real me, I thought. At least *part* of the real me.

I took a deep breath. "I am going to sing," I told Parker quietly. Tossing back my hair, I strode forward. "Hand over that mike!" I told the deejay.

My friends went nuts.

Microphone in hand, I avoided Parker's gaze as I called out, "Any requests?"

"Mariah Carey," someone suggested.

"Bonnie Raitt," someone else said.

"The Beatles," Rox said. "'If I Fell.'"

That's one of my very favorite songs, but it's on the slow side. "Too mellow," I replied. I made myself look at Parker. I'll sing to you if you let me, I pleaded with my eyes.

Parker didn't smile. For a split second I was tempted to drop the mike and walk away. Then my gaze shifted to Stephen, whose whole face was shining with encouragement. "I've got it," I told my audience. "This is by the late, great Janis Joplin. Who's going to play backup? Jeremy, get up here with me!"

The instant I started to sing, I forgot about Parker's disapproval. My voice is a lot like Janis's—gritty, deep, and strong—and I gave the song all I had, filling my lungs and shouting the lyrics. "Take a . . . take another little piece of my heart, now, baby," I sang, tossing back my long hair.

My friends started singing along. I danced as I sang, getting totally into it. "You know you've got it," I sang, and the whole place joined in on, "if it makes you feel good!"

I sang another stanza, then repeated the refrain,

this time throwing in a Janis Joplin–type scream. "You know you've got it—yeah! Take a . . ." The crowd went wild.

When I finished the song, I took a deep bow, my hair flopping forward and brushing the floor. I stood up again, grinning. Mita, Cath, Sully, Rox, Kurt, and Tony were clapping as hard as they could. Stephen was, too.

But the rest of the Seagate crowd—including my boyfriend—had bailed.

Parker was gone.

Eight

"Do you need a ride home?"

It was closing time, and the Rusty Nail was emptying out. I turned to see who had spoken. It was Stephen. "Yeah, I guess so." I stuck my hands in the pockets of my jeans, trying to smile. It was hard—my emotions were all over the place. I'd had a blast singing, but Parker had really hurt my feelings and made me angry, too. "My date left a long time ago, as you may have noticed."

Outside the Rusty Nail, I said good-bye to Cath, Rox, and the others and climbed into the passenger seat of Stephen's car. When Stephen started the engine, a song came on the CD player. "You like Luscious Jackson, too?" I asked as we drove out of the parking lot. "This is one of my favorite CDs."

He nodded. "Their vocalist is almost as good as you."

I slumped down in my seat. "I shouldn't have done it," I mumbled.

"Are you kidding? You were great!"

"But look where it got me." I gestured at his car. "Hitchhiking home."

I couldn't help it—I started to cry. Stephen shot me a worried glance. "Hey, maybe it's not as bad as it seems," he said. "I mean . . ."

"Parker *ditched* me," I reminded him, searching in the glove compartment for some Kleenex. "I just don't get it. How could he do that?"

I blew my nose loudly. Stephen was quiet for a minute. "Parker cares a lot about appearances, how things look, whereas you don't," he said finally. "You two are just . . . different. Maybe opposites attract at first, but in the long run, if you don't see things the same way, it could be for the best if . . ."

My body went cold, then a white-hot flash of anger tore through me. Who does this guy think he is? I thought, throwing the tissue on the floor of the car. "I'm not good enough for Parker, is that what you're saying?" I demanded. "We should break up because he's classy and I'm not?"

"I didn't say that," Stephen said. "That's not what I meant at all."

I folded my arms across my chest, and Stephen gripped the steering wheel tight with both hands, and we sat in stony silence for a while, listening to the Cranberries. I was wishing I'd gotten a ride from Mita and Rox or Cath and Tony instead of Stephen when he remarked, "You really do have a fantastic voice, Rose." He tapped the brakes and pulled into my driveway. "I think it's great that you weren't embarrassed to get up and sing in front of all those people. Seriously."

Is that supposed to make me feel better? I

wondered, even more upset than before. "I guess that's one of the many *differences* between you and me," I pointed out, giving the word he'd used a heavy, sarcastic emphasis. "Just like between me and Parker."

The car hadn't totally stopped yet, but I grabbed the door handle, anyway. "Rose, I didn't mean—," Stephen began.

I got out of the car and slammed the door without waiting for him to finish his sentence and without saying good-bye.

Summer in coastal Maine can feel like winter anyplace else. The next day started out sunny, but over the course of the morning the little white clouds that had speckled the sky multiplied and darkened until they blotted out the blue altogether. Meanwhile the temperature dropped steadily—by lunchtime it was only in the fifties, so I put on a jacket to go to the marina to look for Parker.

I'd waited an hour or two that morning before calling, hoping he'd call me first. When he didn't, I dialed his number with trembling fingers. Mrs. Birtwhistle told me he wasn't home—she thought he'd gone to work on the boat.

I walked fast, trying to beat the rain. I didn't. As I hurried along the dock toward slip nine fat drops began to fall. I folded my arms over my head, trying to keep my hair dry so I wouldn't look like a total wreck when I confronted Parker about why he'd left the Rusty Nail.

But I shouldn't have bothered worrying about how I looked. When I got to the boat, I saw Parker with his arms around another girl. A girl with black, chin-length hair. Valerie.

I felt sick. My experiment showing Parker "the real me" had backfired. He'd found someone who wouldn't embarrass him in public. Someone who wouldn't have to borrow a dress for the prom. I ran back up the dock before they spotted me, dodging the raindrops and trying not to cry. I knew now why Parker had abandoned me—and for whom.

The door to the boutique opened just as I was getting ready to leave at the end of the day. "We're closed," I started to say. Then I saw who it was. "Parker!" I said, surprised.

"Want to grab a bite to eat?" he asked, smiling as if nothing had happened.

I nodded dumbly.

We climbed into the Jeep. "Lousy weather, huh?" he said as he shifted into reverse, ready to back away from the curb.

"Too wet to go sailing?" I asked.

"I worked on the boat but didn't take her out."

I swallowed hard. It was time for the moment of truth. "I know you did," I told him. "I saw you. You and . . . Valerie."

Parker glanced at me. "Yeah?"

"Yeah."

"And . . ."

"You were kissing her," I burst out. "I saw you!"

Parker slid the Jeep back into the parking space. "Val was there," he admitted. "Maybe I gave her a hug or something. We're close—I've never pretended otherwise."

"You said 'on-again, off-again,'" I reminded him. "So which is it?"

"Can we talk about this later?" he asked. "I'm starving."

"I want to talk about it now," I insisted.

"We'll discuss it at a restaurant, okay?"

"Fine," I said sharply. "How about Patsy's?" I suggested, naming the diner where Rox is a waitress.

"That greasy dump?"

"Okay, you pick a place," I retorted.

"Do they serve dinner at the Rusty Nail?" he asked in a sarcastic tone.

I raised one eyebrow. "I don't think so."

"So what was that all about last night?" he asked.

"What was what all about?"

"Your lovely little performance."

"I was trying to have fun," I replied, my face growing warm. "Sorry if I embarrassed you. Not that you stuck around long enough for that."

"I saw enough," he said. "Look, let's not fight. You made a mistake, I made a mistake. They cancel each other out."

I stared at Parker. "You're kidding," I exclaimed. "I sing one stupid song and you cheat on me with another girl and those two things are equal?"

"I'm not cheating on you," Parker insisted. "You're overreacting. Why are we even discussing this?"

I remembered Stephen's comment as he drove me home the night before, about the differences between Parker and me. Stephen had been right. "Maybe we don't have as much in common as we thought," I said quietly.

"It's this dumb job of yours," Parker decided. He gestured to Cecilia's. "It takes up all your time—I hardly ever see you. Why don't you quit?"

The engine was still idling, and the windshield wipers swished back and forth. Did he really just ask me that? I wondered disbelievingly. "I *can't* just quit," I told Parker. "I need the money. I *have* to work."

Parker turned in his seat so we were face-to-face. I looked him straight in the eye and went on talking. "Yeah, isn't that funny? Having to work? But I do. My family's broke—my mom can't support all of us by herself. We're getting food stamps! Isn't that a riot?"

I tried to laugh, but pain closed my throat, choking me. Now he knows, I thought, dropping my eyes. No more secrets.

I looked down at my hands, which were folded on my lap, and waited for Parker to say something comforting, to apologize, to reach out and hold me. Ten seconds passed, then twenty. Finally I looked up at him again.

"Are you serious, Rose?" he said at last.

"Yes, I am."

He wrinkled his forehead. I wanted love and sympathy, but Parker just looked confused. He didn't touch me or speak. He didn't have to—I knew what he was thinking. Since I was pretty, he could forgive me for being a "local" and for going to the public high school. He could even forgive me for singing Janis Joplin at the Rusty Nail. But he couldn't forgive me for being poor.

Tears stung my eyes. "Sorry, Parker. I'm not Val Mathias and I never will be, no matter what dress you put me in," I said quietly.

Neither of us spoke after that. We had nothing left to say to each other. Parker wasn't Prince Charming after all, or maybe I just wasn't cut out to be Cinderella.

Shoving open the door of the Jeep, I jumped down, right into a puddle. It was still pouring and I was instantly soaked to the skin, but I didn't care.

By the time I dried off in the women's room at Patsy's and spilled my sob story to Rox, the downpour had ended and the sun was out again. Everything steamed in sudden warmth.

As I rode my bike slowly home an eerie sort of calm settled over me. Strangely, I didn't feel that upset. It's just shock, I thought. You'll be really upset tomorrow. The words to a very appropriate Gin Blossoms song—"Found Out About You"— kept running through my head.

As I wobbled into the gravel driveway on my

bike I couldn't help singing out loud. Sometimes songs are so much like real life, it's scary.

Then I saw that my three younger sisters were scattered around outside the old barn we use as a garage. Daisy, wearing shorts and a halter top with one of Dad's beat-up caps pulled on over her long blond hair, was trying unsuccessfully to start our old gas-powered lawn mower. Laurel and her pal Jack were busy by the row of chicken wire hutches that Laurel had built recently along the outside of the garage. Lily, dressed in a sailor dress and a straw hat with a trailing blue ribbon, was curled up under a nearby apple tree, writing in a notebook.

So much for sneaking up to my room for a good cry. I decided to hang out with my sisters—maybe they could cheer me up. I wanted to do something that didn't involve talking about Parker for a while.

I joined Daisy. "Are you all right?" she asked, looking closely at my face.

"Fine," I replied, taking a deep breath. "What are you doing, anyway?"

"Isn't it obvious?" Daisy gave the mower's handle one last yank, but the motor still didn't catch. "Broken," she observed unnecessarily.

"Think you can fix it?" I asked as she lugged a toolbox out of the garage.

She inspected the screwdriver collection, choosing a tool carefully. "I'd better be able to." She brushed back a wayward strand of blond hair. "The grass is practically up to my knees. And that reminds me. Aren't you supposed to fix those loose boards on the porch? Everybody keeps tripping."

I grimaced. That was one of the chores Mom had assigned me, unfortunately. "I'm useless with a hammer and nails," I told Daisy. "I'd probably just make it worse. If you do it, I'll take over one of your chores."

"Like fixing the screen door?"

"Well, no. What else have you got?"

She ticked the tasks off on her fingers. "Washing the storm windows, weeding the garden, and reorganizing the pantry."

I seized on the last one as definitely the least grubby and strenuous. "I'll take the pantry," I said. Then I pointed to Lily. "What about Little Miss Muffet over there? I haven't noticed her doing any work."

Daisy shrugged. "She's only eight."

While Daisy fiddled around with the lawn mower, I wandered around the side of the barn, my hands stuck in the pockets of my shorts. Laurel had put Henry back in his cage, and now she was handing Jack a bowl of something that looked like prechewed puppy chow. "Here," Laurel ordered. "Feed the raccoons."

Both of Jack's parents are lawyers, and they're a little bit older. Jack's an only child and he's not a brat, but you can tell just by looking at him that Mr. and Mrs. Harrison treat him like something precious. He was dressed in khakis that actually had creases pressed up the front of the trouser legs. His polo shirt was tucked in and his hair combed neatly over from a dead-straight side part. He looked like a kid from the fifties, like Dick from those old See Spot Run early readers that we have a bunch of on the family room bookshelves.

Anyway, Jack's expression was pretty comical as he took the bowl of disgusting mush from Laurel. Those two were a study in contrasts—Laurel was as grubby as Jack was impeccable. When you're a kid, though, sometimes all it takes to become best friends is living next door to each other—and an interest in animals.

As Jack tentatively offered the mush to the nest of baby raccoons whom he and Laurel had saved— their mother had gotten run over by a car—Laurel stuck some carrot tops into a hutch containing a wild brown rabbit with a tiny splint on one of its paws. I glanced down the row of cages—no vacancy in Laurel's animal hotel. "Since when did you turn into Doctor Dolittle?" I wanted to know.

Laurel shrugged. "I just keep finding animals that need taking care of," she said.

I wrinkled my nose. A musky, zooish smell competed with the cleaner scent of rain-washed grass. "Are you sure it's . . . sanitary?" I bent over to peer into a hutch. A squirrel rose up on its hind legs and chattered angrily at me. I jumped back. "I mean, Henry's almost tame, but don't these wild ones bite? What if they have rabies or something?"

"They don't have any of the symptoms, and I'm supercareful," Laurel said, her eyes flashing.

I decided to keep my distance, anyway. Giving Jack a sympathetic look, I returned to Daisy.

She wasn't alone. Kyle Cooper lives a block away—his sister Maeve's in my class, and he's in Daisy's class. Kyle must have been riding past—he'd dropped his bike on the grass and was leaning against the fence, talking to Daisy, whose face was red from working on the lawn mower. At least I thought that was why it was red. "Well, don't break a fingernail, Daisy," Kyle cracked, his tone sly.

Daisy responded with a dirty look. As soon as Kyle had pedaled off she erupted like a volcano. "What a jerk!" she exclaimed. "I do not grow my fingernails. Can you believe he said that?"

I laughed at her indignation. "He didn't mean anything. He was just flirting with you."

"Flirting? With me?"

I laughed again. "Well, that shirt, Daze. I'm sorry to tell you, it's on the sexy side."

Daisy glanced down at herself, mortified. Suddenly self-conscious about her shape, Daisy hunched her shoulders forward and attacked the lawn mower with renewed energy. I smiled to myself.

I wasn't in any hurry to go inside. Lily was still sitting under the tree, so I called to her, "Hey, Lil, what are you writing?"

Lily clutched her notebook protectively to her chest, as if I had Superman vision and could read it from twenty yards away. Then she jumped to her feet. "None of your business!" she shouted, and darted into the house.

"What's with her?" I wondered aloud.

The sun had dropped behind the trees, and the yard was drenched in warm yellow light. I flung myself down on the grass under the apple tree Lily had just deserted, lying on my back with my arms folded behind my head. Thinking again about Parker, I suddenly realized that instead of being depressed, I felt kind of relieved.

I closed my eyes and let the evening breeze cool my skin. Fall was coming soon. My relationship with Parker was over, and that meant my charade was over as well. I didn't have to pretend anymore. I could be myself. I could hang out at the Rusty Nail with my friends, my real friends, kids who had summer jobs at hardware stores and diners. Back to my imperfect life, I thought . . . and smiled.

Nine

Of course, it didn't take long for my family to find out that I had broken up with Parker.

"Breakfast in bed?" I said. It was a sunny Saturday morning, and I'd been about to jump in the shower when Lily appeared at my door with a tray. "It's not my birthday," I pointed out, yawning. "What's the occasion?"

"I'm just being nice," Lily answered. "Look— it's French toast. I made it myself. And fresh-squeezed orange juice!"

"Wow," I said as she placed the tray on my lap. There was even a wilted daisy in a bud vase. "Lily, that was really sweet of you. Thanks!"

She patted my leg under the blanket in a maternal way. "Now, you just enjoy your breakfast and feel better soon."

The French toast was a little on the soggy side, but I ate every bite. This was so nice of her, I thought, deciding that I'd put off yelling at her about never doing the laundry on time—that was the one chore she'd ended up with after managing to goof up everything else.

Fifteen minutes later I got out of the shower. I

was walking down the hall in my robe, towel drying my hair, when I saw Laurel dart out of my room. "What are you doing?" I called.

"Nothing," she called back with a secretive smile.

I went into my room. While I'd been gone, someone—Laurel, obviously—had made my bed and left a tiny basket on the pillow. I looked inside it. Sitting on a nest of cotton was a little china squirrel.

I turned around. Laurel was peeking around the door to see my reaction. "Do you like it?" she asked.

"It's adorable. But Toad, you shouldn't be spending your piggy bank savings on me."

"I didn't actually spend anything," she confessed. "Jack gave it to me. But I want you to have it," she said quickly when I started to hand the squirrel back to her. "To cheer you up!" she said, disappearing into the hall.

When I carried the breakfast tray downstairs, I was still shaking my head over Lily and Laurel. They were the best sisters in the world!

I took the tray into the kitchen. Daisy was there, washing up the breakfast dishes. "Check out the car," she suggested.

I looked out the window to the driveway, where the station wagon was parked. "Yeah?" I said. "What about it?"

"Check it out," she repeated.

I went to the door, sticking my feet into clogs as

I went. Outside, I folded my arms across the front of my sweater—it was sunny but cool. As I walked over to the car I could see that it was dripping. Someone washed it, I guessed. Daisy. And not only that. The inside was clean, too. She'd thrown out all the trash, and cleaned the upholstery, and vacuumed the floor mats, and washed the windows, and somehow she'd even gotten out the old fish smell.

I went back inside. "Daisy, you are too much," I declared. "Were you scrubbing for hours?"

"Looks like new, doesn't it?" she said, pleased.

I laughed. "Well, that would be pushing it," I said. "But it looks better than it has in years."

"Mom said you can have it all weekend," Daisy told me. "If you want to go to the Rusty Nail or someplace with your friends tonight."

"And if you do go," Mom herself said as she entered the kitchen, "here's something to wear."

She held out a dusty-rose-colored sweater. "Mom, your chenille top," I said. I'd always loved it and had even borrowed it once or twice.

"I think it should be your top." She smiled. "It's your color, after all. And look. I altered the skirt for you. Does the length seem okay?"

I examined the matching skirt. Mom had taken it in at the waist and hemmed it so it would fall just halfway down my thighs. "It's perfect," I exclaimed. "Wait until Rox and Cath and Mita see this outfit! We'll definitely have to go out tonight so I can show it off. I can't wait to—" I stopped.

"Wait a minute. What's going on here? How come everybody's doing such nice things for me?"

"We just thought it should be Be Nice to Rose Weekend," Daisy explained.

"You've been on a bit of an emotional roller coaster the last few months," Mom added. "We want you to head up again and stay up."

I hugged the skirt and sweater to my chest, gazing at my mom and sister with misty eyes. I'd been feeling sorry for myself lately, but it was time to snap out of it. I had a lot to be grateful for. Maybe we don't have money, but our life is rich, I thought. "Thanks, guys," I said. "You're the best."

"Someone's here to see you, Rose," my mother said the next night.

We were all sitting in the family room, watching *Pride and Prejudice* on the public television station. Mom's announcement made my heart jump into my throat. If it was one of my girlfriends, she'd have said the name. But "someone" . . . It might be Parker, I thought, steeling myself for a confrontation.

There was a tall, good-looking guy in khakis and a polo shirt standing just inside the front door, but it wasn't Parker. "Stephen?" I asked, surprised.

He shifted his weight from one foot to the other. "Uh, hi," he said.

I waited for him to explain why he was there. The last time I saw him, we didn't exactly part on friendly terms. When he didn't speak, I said, "What's up?"

"Can we sit outside?" he asked, looking at something over my shoulder.

I turned around. Lily had followed me and was peering around the bend in the hall.

"Sure," I said, ushering Stephen out to the porch and then shutting both the screen door and the inner door so my sister wouldn't be tempted to eavesdrop.

I sat down on the porch swing. Stephen hitched himself onto the railing. He still looked uncomfortable—almost nervous. "Rose, I just wanted to tell you that I heard about you and Parker. And I'm really sorry . . ."

The second he started talking, something in my brain clicked. I'd almost forgotten exactly who Stephen Mathias was.

"You knew all along, didn't you?" I asked him quietly.

"What?" said Stephen, his eyebrows drawn together.

"Valerie's your sister. You had to have known about her and Parker. Why didn't you tell me?" My mind was reeling as I tried to put the pieces of the puzzle together.

"I didn't think it was my place to—"

"You *did* try to tell me . . . ," I said slowly, and the guilty look on his face confirmed my suspicions. "That day at Cecilia's. When you wanted to know what Parker was up to. And that night—in the car, when you told me that Parker and I were different. You were . . . warning me." I laughed harshly. "You must think I'm an *idiot*," I went on. I pushed off from the wood floor with my bare feet, making the swing rock crazily. "I suppose everyone from Seagate knew Parker was seeing Valerie behind my back. Well, you can go back and tell them that I fell for it. I never suspected a thing! Okay?"

"I'm not going to tell anyone anything."

"Oh, come on, Stephen," I said. "What are you here for? To say I told you so? Well, you were right—Parker found someone who isn't so *different* from him, after all. You were so right—I see that now."

"You don't *see* anything," Stephen blurted. "I'm here because I care about you. *That's* why I'm here."

I stopped swinging, my feet planted on the floor. "W-What?" I stammered.

Stephen looked hurt. "Maybe I should have kept my mouth shut. I think I'd better go."

"What?" I asked again, my own face scarlet. What was happening? Stephen cared for me—and now he was leaving? But didn't he think . . . didn't he think we were different? I'd never been so confused. I sat on the swing, not knowing what to do or say.

"Good night," he said, and walked down the steps to the front path.

"Good night," I echoed as he disappeared into his car and drove away.

*   *   *

"What do you mean, you 'accidentally' opened the doors to all seven hutches?" Laurel screeched.

At the same moment Daisy bellowed, "What do you mean, you 'borrowed' my Yaz baseball mitt and now you can't find it?"

It was breakfast time, two weeks after my breakup with Parker. The object of Laurel's and Daisy's wrath was seated at the kitchen table, digging into a huge bowl of Rice Krispies. Not inappropriately, she was dressed in a witch costume complete with tall black hat.

"Those baby raccoons aren't ready to take care of themselves." Laurel was near tears. "How could you?"

"If they really liked you, they wouldn't have run away," Lily replied.

Her hands balled into fists, Laurel stormed out of the kitchen, heading in the direction of her now empty animal B&B. Lily turned to Daisy. "I don't know why you care about that scrungy old thing," Lily said. "It smells."

"You'd better find that mitt," Daisy warned, glaring, "or I'll throttle you, I really will."

Lily's lower lip pushed out in a theatrical pout. "Mom!" she wailed. "Daisy's scaring me!"

Mom was trying to drink a cup of coffee, eat a piece of toast, and read the manual for our malfunctioning dishwasher all at the same time. She paused just long enough to frown at Lily. "Young lady, I don't need trouble from you this early in the day. You know you're not supposed to take your sisters' things without asking first."

"And the mitt's not all," Daisy went on, launching into a list of complaints now that she had Mom on her side. "Last week she broke my favorite—"

"I'm out of here," I sang, pushing back my chair. Lily drove me nuts sometimes, but I didn't feel like sticking around for the rest of her trial. "I'll wash the dishes when I get home from work, Mom. See you."

Compared to the chaos at home, my job at Cecilia's was looking better and better all the time. It's not so bad being sixteen, I thought. If I were only thirteen, like Daisy, I'd have to stay home and take care of Laurel and Lily all day. Ugh!

I had some extra time, so on my way to the boutique I stopped at Wissinger's Bakery for a few doughnuts, then parked my bicycle in front of Appleby's Hardware. The door to the store was propped open with a bag of lawn fertilizer, and Cath was lugging out wheelbarrows, rakes, and other garden tools to make a display on the sidewalk. "Got any hot apple cider to go with these?" I asked her.

"Only if you brought jelly doughnuts," she replied with a smile.

Appleby's always has a pot of hot cider on for the customers—it's one of those old-fashioned kind of stores. Cath filled two plastic foam cups and we sat down on the steps out front, both of us reaching into the greasy bag of still warm doughnuts at the same time.

I had gotten jelly—I knew they were Cath's

favorites. She bit into one, chased it with a slurp of hot cider, then tilted her face up to the morning sun. "This is going to be a good day," she said.

It seemed like a safe prediction. Slouching back with my elbows propped on the step behind me, I sampled a chocolate glazed—my own personal favorite. "I can't believe I'm eating this."

"Why?"

"I already had breakfast at home."

"You'll work it off," Cath said.

"You'll work yours off—I just stand around at my job."

Cath eyed me speculatively. "You have gained a couple of pounds in the last few weeks."

"I have?" I asked, worried.

"It looks good," she asserted. "Your face looks better. You were getting too thin, trying to fit in with Parker's crowd. He was never good enough for you, anyway," Cath declared.

I wanted to hug her, but I would've gotten doughnut crumbs all over her. My friends had been so great since Parker and I had broken up, taking me out every couple of nights, calling to check up on me, doing nice things for me, giving me pep talks. "It's not a question of good enough," I concluded. "He wasn't right for me, that's all."

"You'll meet someone a million times nicer."

"That reminds me." I'd told her and Rox and Mita about my very strange conversation with Stephen. "He called me last night. What's going on with that guy?"

"Duh. He likes you," Cath said.

"But why?"

She raised her eyebrows. "Could it be because you're beautiful, smart, funny, and talented?"

I shook my head. "I just don't get it. I'm not ready to date someone new, anyhow. Especially not another rich preppie."

"Then don't," she advised. "Have another doughnut."

We talked for a few more minutes until the doughnuts and hot cider were gone and my watch told me it was time to hustle over to Cecilia's. I knew Cath was right when she said I looked better—I felt better, too. I was back to my old self, comfortable in my own skin and in my slightly-less-than-the-latest-fashion clothes. And I planned to stay that way.

When I got home that evening, the kitchen smelled like roasting chicken and my mom was sitting at the kitchen table, the newspaper classified section open in front of her and a pen in her hand. "What are you doing?" I asked, dropping into the chair next to her.

"Going through the help-wanted ads."

"Why?"

"Because I hate my job." She circled one ad and scrawled a question mark next to another. Then she threw down the pen. "But the problem is, I'm not qualified for anything else. If I call up these places, they'll ask right off the bat if I have a B.A. and when I say no, they'll say forget it."

"You don't know until you try," I reminded her.

Mom shook her head, sighing. "I'm sorry, Rose. I really am."

"Sorry for what?"

"For this." She spread her hands. "For not being able to find a better job and for shifting so much of the burden onto you and your sisters. Your dad and I should have saved for a rainy day, but we just never expected . . ."

Her voice trailed off, and she rubbed her face with her knuckles. When she lowered her hands again, the delicate, shadowy skin under her eyes glistened with tears.

Guilt pierced my heart as I thought about how I'd blamed Mom for our troubles. It wasn't fair—she was trying her hardest. And I hadn't been helping nearly as much as I could. "It's okay, Mom. Don't worry about me, anyway. I don't mind working at Cecilia's."

She gazed at me, her forehead creased. "You don't?"

"No." And just then I realized something. I wasn't just saying that to make her feel better. It was true. "I like earning my own money. I like doing something productive with my time instead of just hanging out."

She smiled wryly. "Get out of here. Kids love just hanging out."

"Well, then I'm not a kid anymore," I informed her. "I can loaf on my days off like a grown-up.

And you know what else, Mom? Maybe you don't
have a college degree, but you're really smart.
You'll find a good job."

For a moment we just looked at each other. It
was the most we'd talked in months. The role re-
versal was a little weird—here I was, supporting
my mom the way she'd always supported me—but
I didn't mind.

"Thanks for the pep talk," she said.

Leaning forward, I wrapped my arms around
my mother. "Anytime, Mom."

Ten

We were having a big end-of-summer sale at Cecilia's and had been busy all day, so when Stephen came in, I didn't notice him at first. All of a sudden there he was, standing in front of the cash register.

"Can I help you?" I asked. Then I added, "Don't tell me—it's your other grandmother's birthday."

"No, I just have a quick question," Stephen said in a businesslike tone. "When do you get off work?"

"Five-thirty. Why?"

"Just wondering." With that he strode out of the store.

Five-thirty rolled around, and I was slinging my bag over my shoulder when the bell over the door jingled and there was Stephen again. Coincidence? I don't think so.

"On your way home?" he asked.

I couldn't help smiling. "You know I am."

Stephen has a serious expression—when he smiles, it's a pleasant surprise. He smiled now. "Okay, so, another question. Would you like to go for a drive?"

"A drive?" I repeated.

"Yeah. Like, in a car."

"Your car?"

"Sure."

"Where would we go?"

"No place special. Up the coast, maybe. Just for fun. A chance to talk."

"Okay, here's a question for you," I countered. "Why do you like me so much?"

I looked Stephen straight in the eye, my hands on my hips. I wanted an honest answer. If he says that he likes me because I'm pretty, like Parker did, I thought, he's history.

"Because you're beautiful," he said, and I felt like I'd been punched in the stomach. Why did everyone only care how I looked? I opened my mouth to tell him off, but then he interrupted, adding, "The way you're kind even to people who hurt your feelings, and the way you always gave Parker the benefit of the doubt, and the way you aren't afraid to sing in front of a group of people," he said, "is beautiful. I really admire you, Rose. I want to get to know you better."

For a moment I was breathless. "Really?" I choked out finally.

"Really. But it'll only be fun if you want to get to know me better, too."

I nodded. "I think I do." Then, in case I sounded too agreeable, I added, "I mean, you're just going to keep asking until I say yes, right? I'm saving us both a lot of trouble."

"Right," said Stephen, laughing.

We headed north in Stephen's black Saab—the one I'd seen Val drive—taking a country road with views of rocky beaches and lighthouses.

"How long have you lived in Hawk Harbor?" Stephen yelled over the roar of the wind.

"Forever," I yelled back. "How about you?"

"Just a few years. My parents wanted me and Val to go to Seagate—my dad went there—but they didn't want us to board." He flashed me a grin. "Boarding school kids get into too much trouble."

"Your father commutes to Portland?"

"Boston. He just comes home for weekends."

Slowing down, Stephen turned down a side road, which made it easier to talk. "That must be weird, only seeing your father on weekends," I remarked.

Stephen shrugged. "It's better than nothing."

He must have noticed my expression out of the corner of his eye because he stepped on the brakes, almost bringing the Saab to a halt. "I'm sorry, Rose," he said. "That came out wrong—I wasn't thinking. I know about your dad. I was sorry to hear about his fishing accident."

I gave him a sidelong glance. How did he know about my father? I wondered. I guessed he must have asked around. Stephen *wanted* to know about my life, I realized.

"It's just . . ." He accelerated again. "My dad's a workaholic. Even when we all lived in Boston, Val and I hardly ever saw him."

"That's too bad." I was interested in what he

was saying, but I wished he'd stop mentioning his sister. It kept reminding me of how bizarre the connection between us was.

"Maybe we should head back," I said suddenly. "I'm supposed to cook dinner tonight."

"Whatever you want," Stephen said. He looked a little disappointed, though.

As we drove back to Hawk Harbor, Stephen flashed me another one of those surprising grins. "So, Rose, if I turn on the radio, would you sing along?"

"Are you giving me a hard time?" I asked.

"No way. You have a great voice. If you've got it, flaunt it."

"Yeah, well." I had to laugh. "Obviously that's my philosophy, too."

"Do you take singing lessons?"

"Not anymore. I'm in performance choir, though."

"Who's your favorite singer?"

"Do you really want to know?"

He shot a glance at me. "Yeah, I really want to know."

I folded my arms. "Okay, then, guess."

"Um . . ." He was obviously thinking back to the Rusty Nail. "Janis Joplin."

"Nope."

"Uh, Luciano Pavarotti."

I laughed. "Try again."

"Frank Sinatra?"

I groaned. "No, you're right," Stephen decided. "It's probably a woman."

"It's a woman," I confirmed.

"Ani DiFranco? Ella Fitzgerald?"

"Somewhere in between," I said. "Sheryl Crowe."

"How come Sheryl Crowe?"

I thought about it for a moment. "Well, she doesn't have the prettiest voice, but she puts her heart and soul into it. She writes great songs, and she really rocks. That's what I want to do."

"I bet you will someday," he said.

A few minutes later we were parked in my driveway. I kind of wished I hadn't told Stephen to turn around. "So long," I said as I stepped out of the Saab.

"This was a good start," Stephen said.

"A good start to what?"

"Well, I think you're starting to like me a little, aren't you?"

I was. "A little," I told him, and smiled.

Stephen drummed his fingers on the leather steering wheel. "So, Rose. Do you think if I call you again, we could . . . ?"

"Go out for real?" My smile widened. "Try it and see."

He said he'd call, I thought the next day, which was Saturday. So when is he going to call? Today? Tomorrow? Next week? Next month?

As I made myself a sandwich for lunch I told myself I didn't care. The last thing I wanted was to date another guy who went to Seagate. And

Stephen was Valerie's brother . . . we were talking serious bad genes!

Stephen's different, though, I reflected as I spread some of Mrs. Smith's wild blueberry jam on a piece of bread. His family was rich, but he wasn't stuffy and self-centered like Parker. When we talked, he really listened to what I had to say.

I carried my sandwich to the table, where Lily and Laurel were eating clam chowder while Mom thumbed through a pile of cookbooks. "Can't decide what to make for dinner?" I asked her.

"Just getting ideas," she answered, penciling something in the margin of one of the books. "The Schenkels have asked me to cater their fortieth anniversary party, can you believe it? I want to run a menu by Vera this afternoon."

"That's cool," I exclaimed. "And yes, I can believe it. You're the best cook in Hawk Harbor, Mom."

"Well, I don't know about that," she said modestly. "It'll be a challenge cooking for thirty people instead of just my family." She sounded a little worried, but at the same time she smiled—I hadn't seen her eyes sparkle like that in a long, long time. "It'll be fun, though."

Just then there was a muttered curse from Lily. She was scribbling in a notebook while she slurped her soup, and she'd splashed clam chowder all over the page. "Watch your language," Mom warned her.

"What are you writing?" I asked.

Lily wiped the paper with her napkin. "A story," she said.

"What about?"

"Nothing." Lily stuck the notebook under her arm and grabbed her soup bowl. "I'm done."

"Wait a minute," said Laurel. "Isn't it your turn to empty the dishwasher and clean up the kitchen?"

"I'm busy," Lily responded, darting from the kitchen before anyone could stop her.

"Well, I'm busy, too." Laurel pushed back her chair. "I'm going over to Jack's. Mr. and Mrs. Harrison are taking us to—"

Laurel stopped. Daisy had just entered the room. "What?" asked Daisy, putting a hand to her head self-consciously. "Why are you staring?"

"Your hair!" Laurel exclaimed.

The last time I'd seen Daisy, her glossy blond hair fell almost to her waist. Now her hair was so short, you could practically see her scalp.

Daisy looked as if she were about to cry. "It was just getting in the way," she said, trying to sound tough. "How could I mow lawns and weed gardens and stuff with stupid long hair falling in my face all the time?"

I was about to ask her if this had anything to do with Kyle Cooper when the phone rang. I jumped up to answer it, my heart jumping, too.

But it wasn't for me. I held the phone out to Daisy. "For you," I told her. I mouthed a name. "Kyle."

Her face flaming, Daisy grabbed the phone, then retreated as far as the tautly stretched cord would allow. I tried to eavesdrop but couldn't hear her because Laurel was talking to Mom. "This really neat kids' museum in Portland," she was saying. "The Harrisons are members, so they get in free. And we'll probably go out for ice cream—Mr. Harrison loves hot fudge sundaes. And if there's time, Mr. Harrison said we could go for a ride on this cool old-fashioned steam train. Oh, I won't be home for dinner—I'm eating at Windy Ridge tonight."

Before Mom could get a word in edgewise, Laurel whisked out the door. At the same instant Daisy slammed down the telephone. "What did Kyle want?" I asked.

"He asked me *out!*" Daisy fumed.

"And that's a crime?" I said.

"Did you say yes?" Mom wanted to know.

"Of course not!" Daisy yelled.

"But why?" I teased. "Your hair's really not so bad. With a little styling gel . . ."

Daisy burst into angry tears and stomped out of the room. "Rose," my mother chastised me.

"With that haircut she'd better learn to take a joke," I replied. I could see Lily still lurking in the hall. "Are you getting all this down?" I called to her. "Great story material!"

The phone rang again. "It's probably Vera," Mom guessed.

"Or Kyle," I said. "He's the persistent type." I picked up the receiver. "Hello?"

"May I speak to Rose?" asked Stephen.

Mom gave a knowing smile as my face lit up. "Speaking," I said.

Why did I agree to go out with him? I agonized just six hours later.

When Stephen asked me out to dinner, I'd assumed we were talking pizza or fried clams. Instead I found myself seated across from him at an intimate table for two at the Harborside, the very same restaurant where Parker had hosted my sixteenth birthday and taken me before the prom bash back when we were a couple.

Stephen was wearing khakis, a white oxford shirt, and a tie—he was dressed way more formally than Parker ever had been except when we went to the prom. My short denim jumper, T-shirt, and sandals, which had seemed cute at home, now seemed way too casual. I was having a Parker flashback—another one of those when-worlds-collide moments.

I opened the menu, telling myself not to feel stupid just because Stephen was dressed better than I was. "Wow, everything sounds good," I murmured, checking out the catch of the day. And expensive!

"If you don't like seafood, the steak is good, too," Stephen said. "I'm thinking about the swordfish myself."

I was thinking about ordering a plain green salad just in case we ended up splitting the check.

Now I arched one eyebrow at Stephen. "Are you trying to impress me?" I asked.

Stephen fumbled with his menu, nearly knocking over his water glass. "No. Why? I just thought you'd like the food here. I mean, it's . . ."

"The fanciest restaurant in Hawk Harbor," I filled in. "We're the only people under thirty in the whole place!"

Stephen grinned. I was glad—I liked that grin. "Okay, guilty as charged. I am trying to impress you. Does that make me a jerk?"

"I guess not," I said, smiling.

"But you'd rather have a burger and fries."

"Sort of," I admitted.

"Then that's what you'll get."

I looked at the menu, confused. "But I don't think the Harborside serves—"

Stephen was refolding his cloth napkin. "Come on," he hissed. "Let's go!"

A minute later we were in the parking lot, laughing hard. "It's okay," Stephen assured me. "We hadn't even ordered. They can't arrest us."

"But I drank from my water glass," I gasped, giggling. "I touched the silverware!"

"You're right. That's a felony in the state of Maine," Stephen joked. He tossed his car keys in the air. "So, the ball's in your court, Ms. Walker. Where to?"

We ended up at Cap'n Jack's, which has the best burgers in town as well as the cheapest, freshest lobster. "My dad used to sell fish to this restaurant," I told Stephen as we dug into a basket of Cap'n Jack's famous onion rings.

"No kidding," he said. "What kind of fish did he catch?"

"Cod, halibut, flounder."

"Did he like it, fishing? I mean, was it a good way to make a living?"

I thought about Mom and the classified ads, about the humiliation of food stamps, about how she and Dad somehow never managed to save for a "rainy day." Then I pictured my father coming home at the end of the day, his smile gleaming in a face brown from the sun, how he'd grab me for a bear hug and his arms would smell like the ocean. "Yeah, he liked it," I replied, my throat suddenly tight with tears. "He liked working outdoors, and he was proud to be his own boss. He was a happy man."

I'd never talked to Parker like this—I must have known instinctively that he wouldn't understand, or wouldn't care, which would have been worse.

Stephen reached across the table and squeezed my hand. "You must really miss him," he said.

I nodded, not trusting myself to speak.

"Did you ever go out on the boat with him?"

I took a deep breath and had to smile at the memory. "I'll never forget the very first time," I told Stephen. "I was about Lily's age—eight or nine. Anyway, we went out to the banks, and Dad was pretty sure we were over a big school of cod, so he set the nets. And there was a ton of fish, so when he pulled up the nets they were all over the deck of the boat, jumping around and totally scary—I mean, it hadn't occurred to me they'd be *alive*, you know? I started to cry—we're talking major hysterics—so there's Dad, in the middle of the Atlantic with a boat full of cod, sitting on the gunwale with me on his lap, calming me down and telling me not to be afraid of the fish."

We were both laughing. Just then Stephen's lobster came. He held up the plastic bib that came with it. "I've only ordered lobster a couple of times before, and it's always been cut up in a salad or something," he confessed. "You're a fisherman's daughter. Do I really have to wear this?"

"Yep. And lose the tie while you're at it," I advised.

We ate so much at Cap'n Jack's, we decided to go for a walk on the beach afterward. It was a beautiful August night—the full moon made the beach almost as bright as day. "Want to take a swim?" I asked Stephen.

Stephen walked up to the water's edge, jumping back when a wave washed over his bare feet. "Are you nuts?" he yelped. "It's like ice."

I laughed. "You're not a native, are you?"

"Hey, I took off the necktie," he said. "That's all I'm taking off."

We walked down the beach, just below the high-tide line, where the seaweed piles up. I felt incredibly relaxed around him, as if we'd been taking

moonlit walks on the beach forever. He's such a
sweet guy, I thought, a little bit giddy. How come I
never realized that?

"So, how are the eighth graders?" I asked.

He sighed. "They're okay. The program I work
with is for underprivileged kids, so a lot of them have
rough home lives. Sometimes they take their problems
out on each other, which makes coaching them hard."

"I can imagine."

"Hard but rewarding," he amended. He looked
at me. "I can't wait to graduate next year. I'm
going to take a year off before college and work
with the kids full-time. I just wish I could do more
for them, you know?"

I didn't know what to say. After a minute
Stephen took my hand. "Is this okay?" he asked.

"Sure," I said casually, hoping he couldn't tell
that his touch made me tingle.

"Because I don't want to rush things," he explained. "In case you're still—"

"It's been a few weeks," I reminded him.
"What about you and . . . Camilla, right?"

He laughed. "We broke up almost a year ago."
I looked at him expectantly. "You want details?"
he asked.

"Sure." I smiled. "I mean, you know all the dirt
on me and Parker!"

"Fair enough," Stephen said. "Let's see.
Camilla left for Williams last September first, and I
think it was, like, a whole day later that she called
and broke up with me."

"On the phone?"

"Harsh, right?"

"What was she like?" I asked.

"She was smart," Stephen replied. "She read all the time—books, newspapers. You know, the analytical type. We'd go to a movie and then talk about it for hours."

"That sounds nice," I said, secretly a little jealous. A vague doubt entered my mind. Camilla sounded like the polar opposite of me—I wondered how Stephen could have been interested in both of us. "Do you miss her?"

"I did for a while." He glanced meaningfully at me. "Not anymore."

Too soon, it was eleven o'clock. I didn't want the evening to end, and that surprised me. "You'd better take me home. I have a curfew," I told Stephen apologetically.

"That's cool," he said. "Your mom cares."

"It's because she doesn't know you," I explained. "I mean, you could be a real creep."

"I could be," he agreed. "So, am I?"

I shook my head. I had to admit to myself that I'd really misjudged him. Parker had turned out to be a creep, and so were most of his Seagate friends, but Stephen was different. "No," I said softly, "you're not."

Back at my house he parked the Saab, then came around to open my door. We walked up to the porch and stood for a few seconds, not quite looking at each other. Finally Stephen cleared his throat. "Thanks for going out with me, Rose," he said. "I really enjoyed this evening."

"Me too."

"Would it be okay if I . . . kissed you good night?"

I nodded.

Stephen hesitated, then placed his hands gently on my shoulders. I put one hand on his waist so we'd be balanced. I closed my eyes, and our lips met with one of those little bumps that happen when it's the first time.

We stepped apart again. "Good night, Rose," he whispered.

"Good night," I whispered back.

He jogged down the steps. When he was behind the wheel of the car, I pushed open the door to the house. I was feeling a little bit dizzy. I hadn't expected to stay out this late, to have so much fun, to like Stephen so much. What am I doing? I thought. Am I crazy? Didn't getting burned by Parker teach me anything? Stephen and I are bound to be as different as Parker and I were.

I will not fall for Stephen, I told myself. I will not, I will not.

But I'd wanted that kiss to last a whole lot longer. Ready or not, I *was* falling.

Eleven

"He invited himself over for dinner tonight," I told Rox over the phone. It was the last day of summer vacation. "He says he wants to get to know my family!"

"That's good," Rox said.

"No, it's not. My family's crazy."

"Eccentric," Rox corrected.

"Whatever." I remembered the few times I'd gotten Parker together with my family, even for just a minute or two. Talk about oil and water. "Compared to Stephen's family, they're just not normal."

"Val's normal?"

"Well, no. She's evil. But his little sister, Elizabeth, is a sweetheart, and his mom's really nice. I haven't met his dad yet."

"Just relax," Rox advised me. "You have absolutely no reason to feel insecure."

"You're right," I said.

And she was. Stephen and I had gone out on two more dates and had a great time. I was starting to think of us as a couple. It's just dinner, I reminded myself as I hurried downstairs to see if

Mom needed help in the kitchen. What could go wrong?

Everything, I decided thirty seconds later when I spotted Lily in the family room, wearing Mom's silk bathrobe and a feather boa and reciting Hamlet's "To be or not to be" soliloquy to an appreciative audience composed of Laurel and Henry the mouse.

"Okay, Lily, Laurel, and Daisy," I shouted. "Gather round."

Daisy had been in the kitchen. She stuck her head into the family room. "What's up?"

"As you all know, Stephen's coming over for dinner," I began, ready to launch into the same lecture I'd given them before Parker's arrival on prom night. "So I want you to . . ."

My sisters waited, their eyes round and expectant. Even Henry seemed to be listening. Suddenly I felt like a rodent myself. What am I doing? I thought. I thought about my prom night lecture. It hadn't really made a difference—Parker didn't even pay attention to my sisters. I remembered how sweet my sisters had been when I broke up with Parker. That breakup taught me a lot. Just as I'd discovered that I didn't want to change for Parker or anybody, I didn't want my sisters to change, either. I didn't need Lily to dress like everybody else, and Daisy looked great with a mohawk, and so what if Laurel smelled like a barn?

"Be at the table on time," I finished.

"That's all?" Daisy asked.

"No problem," Lily said, tossing the feather boa over one shoulder.

"Sure. I just need a few minutes to put Henry back in his cage and feed the baby fox I found the other day," Laurel said.

So that was where we left it. My sisters were going to do their own thing. And I'm not going to worry, I told myself.

Dinnertime rolled around, and even though it was a cool evening, I started sweating. I felt like I was on an antiperspirant commercial. All my resolve not to worry about what my sisters did evaporated the minute the doorbell rang.

And from the minute he arrived, Stephen did everything right—and my family did everything wrong.

He brought my mom a big bunch of flowers and a bag of fresh herbs. "Thank you, Stephen," Mom said, sniffing a bunch of basil. "This is my favorite."

"My mom likes to garden," he explained.

Just then Daisy entered the kitchen, bouncing a basketball. When she saw Stephen, her eyes glimmered mischievously. "Hey, catch!" she shouted, and fake-pumped the ball at him.

Daisy laughed as Stephen gave a startled jerk.

"Do you have to be so rude, Daze?" I asked testily.

"No, that's cool," Stephen said with a grin. "You won't catch me off guard next time."

"I'm Daisy," she told him. "Nice to meet you."

"Same here," Stephen said.

"What's cooking?" she asked, turning to our mom.

"Lasagna," Mom told her. "Would you set the table, Daisy?"

"And wash your hands first," I said.

Daisy tucked the ball under her arm. "Why don't you set the table yourself, Miss Picky?"

"Because I'm making salad dressing with the fresh herbs Stephen brought."

"Stephen, have a seat," Mom invited him, gesturing to a stool at the counter, "and tell me about your plans for fall term at Seagate."

While Stephen charmed Mom, I sliced tomatoes and agonized silently about which of my sisters would cause a scene at the table. Why hadn't I read them the riot act? When we were all seated, though, and Mom was serving the food, it looked for a moment as if the meal might go smoothly. Daisy had washed up, and Laurel hadn't looked this clean in years—her hair was actually brushed back into a neat ponytail. Lily had traded the robe and feather boa for denim shorts and a scallop-edged pink T-shirt.

"The lasagna is delicious," Stephen said.

"It's a simple recipe," Mom replied, but she looked pleased.

"Mom cooks a lot," Lily piped up. "She catered this big party the other night, and it was so good, a bunch of other people have hired her to cater parties."

Lily's voice was perky and proud. Stephen flashed her a big smile; I wanted to kick her. She would have to bring up the catering, I thought. Having a mother who's a good cook isn't necessarily a plus. I wondered whether Stephen was drawing a comparison to his own family. They had "help"—Mrs. Mathias only cooked when she felt like it.

Stephen talked to Daisy for a few minutes about the Red Sox—I could tell Daisy was impressed by how many stats he knew. Then he turned to Laurel. "I hear you like animals," he remarked.

As if on cue, a small brown field mouse darted across the table right next to the basket of garlic bread. Stephen jumped, dropping his fork with a clatter. I screamed.

Laurel grabbed Henry, stuffing him back in the pocket of her windbreaker. "Excuse me," she muttered.

"Excuse you?" I yelped. "Toad, I'm going to kill you! I can't believe you brought him to the dinner table!"

"Please take Henry back to the hutch outside, Laurel," Mom said calmly. "You know the rules."

As Laurel pushed back her chair Henry hopped out again. For two exciting minutes

Daisy, Laurel, and Lily all scrambled around under the table trying to recapture him. When Lily let out a triumphant shriek—"Got him!"—I dared a glance at Stephen. He looked as if he were trying not to laugh; I was trying not to cry.

Laurel carried the mouse back outside, and the rest of us resumed eating—not that I had much of an appetite after the Henry episode. Lily started swinging her feet, kicking the rungs of her chair. "Do you like horror movies?" she asked Stephen.

"You bet," he said.

"Okay, well, I'm trying to write a really scary story. Do you think the main character should die by being torn to pieces by a zombie, or be decapitated by an ax murderer, or have his blood sucked out and his heart and eyes gouged out by a vampire?"

"Lily, that's gross," I exclaimed.

"Not to me," she declared. "I think it's interesting. And so does Stephen, right, Stephen?"

"I like vampires myself," he said to Lily. "Have you read *Dracula*?"

"No, but I've seen the movie," she replied.

Lily continued to toss out gruesome story ideas, as if Stephen had agreed to be her literary agent or something. Daisy must have sensed that I was about to strangle Lily because as soon as there was a lull in the conversation, she turned to Stephen and said, "So, how about some one-on-one after dinner?"

They really did play basketball, so by the time Stephen and I were alone, sitting on the porch swing, his oxford shirt was damp with sweat.

"I'm really sorry about the hoops workout," I told him, trying to read his expression.

"Are you kidding? It was fun," he said easily.

That's just his prep school manners talking, I thought, still worried. "And *dinner.*" I shuddered. "You know, my sisters never act like that. Really. It must be a full moon tonight or something."

"I like your sisters," Stephen said.

"They're embarrassing."

"They're funny."

I shook my head, unconvinced. "You're just saying that to be nice."

"I don't say things just to be nice," Stephen told me. "Well, okay, maybe sometimes, but not to you. I really do like your family, Rose." He turned toward me. "Almost as much as I like you."

As Stephen wrapped his arms around me my worries faded. Of course he meant what he said, and I liked him, too. A lot. In fact, I was almost starting to think that this time it might be love, real love.

Stephen's warm lips touched mine, spreading heat throughout my body. I had just managed to calm down when Stephen pulled away in order to give me a big smile. "I wanted this to be a surprise—I was going to tell you tomorrow, when I introduce you—but I can't wait."

"Tell me what? Introduce me to whom?" I asked.

"Marilyn Hopper, the soprano. Have you heard of her? She's a friend of my parents. She's performing for a few months with the Portland Symphony. And guess what? She's willing to give you voice lessons for free!"

I wrinkled my forehead. "What?"

"I told her about you and about what a great voice you have," Stephen explained, "and she said she'd take you on as a student, once a week in Portland, for free since you're a special friend of the family. Isn't that awesome?"

I stared at Stephen, speechless.

"I thought you'd be happy about this." Stephen frowned, apparently puzzled by my silence. "I mean, that's the point, to make you happy."

I'd always dreamed about taking private voice lessons, but for some reason this unexpected gift didn't make me happy. "You mean, my voice isn't good enough the way it is," I stated flatly.

"Your voice is fine," Stephen said. "It's like anything, though. You have raw talent, but with the right training you could be a star. I mean, I know your family can't afford voice lessons. It's a great opportunity, Rose."

With the right training . . . your family can't afford . . . Stephen's words screamed in my mind like a rising alarm. Does he think I'm some kind of *charity case?* I wondered. That he can *fix me* by

giving me something that my family can't afford?
All of a sudden I wasn't hearing Stephen's voice
and seeing Stephen's face—it was Parker sitting
next to me, Parker telling me that with the right
dress I'd be the prettiest girl at the Seagate
Academy prom, and of course he could arrange
everything. Parker making it clear in countless
little ways that I wasn't good enough the way I
was, that I was rough around the edges.

I'm such an idiot. Why did I think that everything was okay? I wondered. No matter how nice
Stephen was, there was no getting around the
fact that we were different—just like he'd said so
long ago after the Rusty Nail. He had just confirmed all my worst fears. He feels sorry for me, I
thought, horrified. Well, he didn't need to feel
sorry for me. I didn't need his help. My *family*
didn't need his help.

"I don't want to sing with a symphony," I said
aloud. Angry tears stung my eyes. "I'm not an
opera soprano. Don't you get it?"

"What are you talking about?" he asked.
"Look, just come over tomorrow and meet her—"

"Come over? And have dinner with you and
Val?" I demanded, and the sneer in my voice
made me cringe.

"What does Val have to do with anything?"

"You think my sisters and I are hicks, and it's
up to you to change us—"

"I don't want to change you," he broke in,
looking more confused than ever. "I love you."

"You can't love me if you don't appreciate me for the way I am," I insisted. "You said it yourself that night after the Rusty Nail. We belong to different worlds. You'll never loosen up enough to fit in with my family, and I'll never be polished enough to fit in with yours."

"Whoa, hold on. Five minutes ago I was shooting baskets with your sister. If that's not loose enough for—"

I wasn't listening. I knew that no matter what Stephen said, he would never be able to accept me for who I really was. I would never be like Val, and I would never be like Camilla.

Jumping down from the swing, I shouted, "This is never going to work! You can forget about the voice lessons. You can forget about everything!"

I didn't feel like going back inside right then, so I hid out by the garage until the sound of the Saab's engine faded into the night. Then I realized I was shivering. Fall was coming. The night air was cool, and I was wearing only a sundress.

Still dazed by what had just happened, I went inside through the back door. I thought I'd make it to my room without running into anybody, but no such luck. Mom, Laurel, Lily, and Daisy ambushed me at the foot of the stairs.

"Stephen's great," Daisy declared, as if someone had asked her opinion. "Did you see him sink that three pointer?"

"He was so much nicer than that icky Parker," Lily agreed. "I want to show him some of my stories. Can I, Rose?"

"Let's invite him over for dinner again tomorrow night," Laurel said.

"I liked him a lot," Mom told me. She was beaming. "And your father would have, too."

At that I burst into tears.

"What's wrong, Rose?" Mom asked.

"Where is Stephen, anyway?" Daisy wanted to know. "Why'd he leave so early?"

"Because I just broke up with him!" I wailed.

Twelve

"C heer me up," I begged my friends.

What a way to start my junior year—in a major depression. A few days after the breakup I was eating lunch in the high school cafeteria with Rox, Cath, and Mita.

"You want jokes?" Mita asked.

"Anything," I said. It had been really hard to refuse all of Stephen's phone calls after we broke up, but I thought we ought to make a clean break. Still, I was exhausted from all the crying I had been doing.

Mita told a couple of really lame knock-knock jokes. They were so bad, they were almost humorous. Cath and Rox laughed—I smiled, but only a little. "Okay, how about making a list," Rox suggested as she unwrapped her tuna sandwich. "The top ten advantages to not having a boyfriend. Who wants to start?"

"I've got one," Cath volunteered, waving a french fry. "You can dance with anyone you want at parties."

"No more waiting by the telephone for That Certain Someone to call," Rox contributed.

"You don't have to shave your legs as often," said Mita, "and if you forget to put on deodorant, who cares?"

"You have more time for your girlfriends," Cath said.

"You have more time for everything," Mita said.

"More time to be lonely," I said glumly. The fact was, I missed Stephen. Did I make a mistake? I wondered briefly. No, I had to stick to my resolve. Stephen will find a Seagate girl, someone like Camilla, I thought, and I'll end up with a South Regional boy and that will be that.

Cath patted my hand. "It'll get better," she promised.

I nodded. Inside, though, I wasn't so sure. I'd bounced back pretty fast after Parker, but not this time.

I just couldn't stop thinking about Stephen.

Later, on a chilly October afternoon, my family visited my dad's grave. Gray clouds scudded across the sky and a cold northeast wind raked the landscape, twisting the gold and red leaves off their stems and making them fall in showers.

As we stood in front of the simple headstone, a sad silence fell over us. Mom placed a pot of bright yellow mums on the grave, then touched the stone lightly before straightening up again. "It's been a while since we were all here together," she said at last, just the tiniest quaver in her voice. "Does anyone want to say something, to share a memory about Dad?"

"I want to know why Laurel isn't here," Daisy spoke up. She wiped a tear from her eye. "Isn't this important to her?"

There had been a scene when Laurel announced that she was going apple picking with the Harrisons instead of going to the cemetery. Now Mom sighed. "I wish she were here with us, too, but Laurel needs to do what feels right to her."

At that moment Lily started to cry. "I don't like the cemetery," she sobbed, her face hidden in her small hands. "Dad's not here. I want to go home."

Mom knelt down and wrapped her arms around Lily. She looked up at me and Daisy, her eyes questioning. I nodded. "It is kind of cold," Mom decided. "Yes, let's head back."

When we got home, the old Victorian house felt almost as cold as the outdoors. "How about a fire in the fireplace?" Mom suggested, rubbing her hands together. "And maybe some hot cider?"

While Daisy built a fire, I helped Mom in the kitchen. By the time we reappeared with a plate of gingersnaps and four steaming mugs of cider, Lily had disappeared. "She went up to her room," Daisy said, reaching for a cookie. "I guess she wants to be alone."

Mom kicked off her black flats and settled down on the couch, tucking her feet up under her. Daisy curled up next to Mom, draping the afghan over both their knees. I took the rocking chair. For a minute we were quiet, sipping our hot cider.

Daisy broke the silence first. "I remember a day kind of like this, last fall. It was really cold, and I had an away soccer game. Dad drove all the way to Kent with a huge thermos of hot chocolate and a couple dozen doughnuts, enough for the whole team."

"Dad liked doing things like that," I recalled. "Remember how he'd put on magic shows and stuff for our birthday parties?"

"And the time he got the whole neighborhood organized to go Christmas caroling," Daisy said.

I laughed. "I thought I would die of embarrassment over those elf costumes he made us all wear."

Just then a draft of chilly air snaked into the living room. The front door slammed, and Laurel peeked in at us. "Hi," she said.

"Sit down," Mom invited.

Laurel hesitated, then came in and perched on the arm of the sofa. "What are you doing?" she asked.

"We're telling stories about Dad," I answered.

"It's your turn," Daisy said to Laurel.

Laurel was still wearing her jacket, and now she hunched her shoulders, tucking her chin in the collar. "I can't think of anything," she mumbled.

"Come on," I urged. "How about the time Mom was mad at you for sliding down the banister, but you kept doing it, anyway, so Dad rigged that buzzer on the newel post and it went off when you got to the bottom and scared you to death?"

Laurel couldn't help smiling. "That's not funny,"

she said, although you could tell that she thought it was. "I fell off!"

"Dad was always doing goofy things," Daisy said. "Remember that time he made jelly bean and hot dog pizza?"

"And the pancakes shaped like bunnies and stars and boats," said Laurel.

I laughed. "He was *not* a good cook."

"He was a good storyteller, though," said Daisy. "Remember how he used to tell us fairy tales at bedtime, only he'd make us the characters?"

My sisters and I talked until the cider and cookies were gone and the fire had burned down to glowing embers. "You know, Lily was right," Daisy said at one point. "At the cemetery, when she said Dad wasn't there. He's here." Daisy waved a hand. "In all these rooms. In our memories. In us."

We sat quietly, thinking about this. It was true. The house still felt like Dad in so many ways. He was in the kitchen, flipping pancakes on a Sunday morning; he was out in the barn, repairing his nets; he was upstairs in the hallway at bedtime, checking each of our rooms in turn to make sure we were tucked in and sleeping peacefully. During his life he'd always been there, making us feel safe. Dad took care of us, but he also helped us do things on our own. He talked me out of my stage fright before a concert and played endless games of catch with Daisy when she wanted to try out for the boys' Little League team, and he told Laurel she could still climb trees even if she couldn't slide down banisters, and he never laughed when Lily came to the dinner table dressed like Daniel Boone.

I thought about how I hadn't wanted to tell Parker about my dad, about how I had been ashamed that he was a fisherman. Now I was ashamed that I'd ever felt that way. Dad had been honest and generous and steadfast. He'd believed in me—in all of us. Talking about Dad made my heart ache with longing—I knew I'd never stop missing him. But I knew, too, that if I let it, his spirit would always stay with me.

There'd always be an inner voice saying, I believe in you, Rose.

Thirteen

Fall passed quickly, and the days grew darker and shorter.

November is the gloomiest month of the year, I thought one Saturday afternoon as I drove down Old Boston Post Road.

When I saw the sign for the social services center, I tapped the brakes and turned into the parking lot. For a minute I sat with my hands gripping the steering wheel, seriously wishing I hadn't volunteered to pick up the month's food stamps. Then I gave myself a little kick in the pants. "Grow up for once, Rose Walker," I mumbled.

I went inside the building, sort of slouching into my oversize U. Maine sweatshirt. I was surprised to see a bunch of people, some waiting in line at the counter and some sitting on orange plastic chairs. For some reason I thought I'd be the only person there, like my family was the only one in the county with problems. How self-centered can you get?

I stood behind a woman who didn't look much older than me. She was holding a baby girl in a pink fleece snowsuit balanced on her hip. A toddler stood next to her, the little girl's skinny arms wrapped around her mother's blue-jean-clad legs.

It was her turn at the counter. "How are you doing, Jane?" the social worker asked her with a warm smile.

The woman shifted the baby to her other hip. "Rick's still out of work," she said in a broad Maine accent. She sounded beat. "And both kids just got over the flu. Some days I wonder how we'll make it until next summer."

The woman behind the counter reached out and touched the young mother's arm. "You'll make it," she said firmly. "You're not alone."

I turned away, a little embarrassed at witnessing such a personal moment. My gaze roamed around the room. Some of the people waiting for help looked like the people who lived on the farms inland from the coast. There were some farm kids at South Regional with me, and I knew farming for them was a tough way to make a living. I can't believe I ever moaned and groaned about not having enough money for clothes and CDs, I thought. My life could be so much worse.

When I faced forward again, the baby was watching me. Her nose was runny, and she wasn't as chubby as babies should be, but when I smiled at her, she smiled back. The baby's mother turned to leave. Her eyes met mine. I smiled again. "Hi," I said.

Her expression was tired and hopeless, but her lips curved up just a little bit. "Hi," she replied.

I stepped up to the counter—it was my turn. "I'm Rose Walker," I told the social worker. My voice was clear and strong.

On the way home I stopped in town to do some more errands for Mom. Main Street seemed subdued—about a third of the stores and almost all the restaurants were closed for the winter. Hawk Harbor was hibernating and, as snowflakes stung my cheeks, I wished I could, too.

I pushed through the door of the Down East News and Drugstore just as someone else was leaving.

Someone else who happened to be Stephen Mathias.

"Rose!" he exclaimed.

"Stephen!" I said.

We stood awkwardly in the doorway, half in and half out. "Uh, here," he said, holding the door. I scurried into the store, and he followed.

We took up neutral positions on either side of a rack of postcards. "So," I said. "Doing some shopping?"

Stephen held up a paper bag. "Toothpaste."

"Hey, I'm shopping for toothpaste, too. So," I said again, wishing I could think of a way to make this toothpaste conversation last forever.

"What's new?" he asked.

"Not a lot." I picked out a postcard with a picture of a giant lobster on it and started idly reading the caption on the back. "You know, school. Concert choir."

"The usual for me, too," he said. "Classes. Sports. I'm studying pretty hard this semester. I'm not going out much," he added, his tone significant.

It was a pretty broad hint, and I blushed as the meaning sank in. He's not dating anybody, I guessed.

For some reason that knowledge made me ridiculously happy, but I tried not to make it too obvious. "Yeah, well, you're a senior now. You have to get serious if you want to get into a decent college."

"Right." He looked at me a moment. "Hey, how about grabbing a cup of cider somewhere?"

The invitation sounded casual, but I knew it wasn't. Sitting down across from each other at Patsy's Diner would be completely different from bumping into each other in the drugstore. Why start something that can only end badly? I thought.

Even so, it was an effort not to say *yes, yes, yes.*

"I've got to do these errands for my mom," I said instead. "Maybe some other time."

He couldn't hide his disappointment, or maybe he just didn't try. For a moment the longing in his eyes was unmistakable. "Some other time," he echoed.

"See you around," I said.

He smiled faintly. "Sure."

Without looking back, Stephen walked out of the store and disappeared into the dusk.

Still clutching the lobster postcard, I wandered

to the toothpaste aisle. I knew what brand Mom wanted, but for the longest time I just stood there, staring blankly at rows of rectangular boxes. I wasn't seeing the toothpaste—I was remembering the look in Stephen's eyes. Now, belatedly, a similar longing washed over me. I wanted to run after him, to touch his hand, to see him smile when I said I'd changed my mind, let's have a cup of coffee. He's really sad, after all this time, I thought. Maybe I was wrong about him. Maybe he really did care.

But I knew that it was too late. I could never make things right with Stephen again. All I could do was stand there in the toothpaste and mouth-wash section of the Down East News and Drugstore, wondering if I'd made a terrible mistake letting him go.

"Where's my black ribbed turtleneck?" I yelled down the hall on Sunday morning. "Lily!"

Lily was supposed to fold the clean laundry and distribute it to everyone's room. I'd cut her some slack for a while, but it was getting ridiculous. "How come I have no clean clothes?" I grumbled to myself. "Lily!"

I stomped down to my sister's room. She had to be hiding the laundry somewhere. Lily wasn't in her room, though, and neither was my black turtle-neck. But I did spot a tattered cardboard binder. Her notebook, I thought.

I knew I shouldn't, but I couldn't help myself. Sitting down on her bed, I opened the notebook and started reading a story that Lily had titled "Dark Days."

The story was only six pages long, but the problems were piled high for Linda, the fatherless eight-year-old heroine. First Linda's family was flung into poverty, then her mother got sick and died, and finally the orphaned child was separated from her three older sisters and sent to live with cruel foster parents.

No wonder Lily has bad dreams, I thought. I had spent so much time getting annoyed with Lily for being rude or neglecting her chores that I had forgotten she was just a little kid. A scared, sad little kid.

Just as I was starting the next story, called "The Zombie's Bloody Revenge," Lily danced into the room wearing a pink ballerina's tutu. She spotted me with the notebook. "What are you doing?" she screeched. "Give me that!" She snatched the notebook from me. "You better not have looked inside it, Rose Annabelle Walker!" she cried, her blue eyes flashing.

"I did look inside," I confessed.

Lily stamped a foot. "Can't you read?" She held the notebook up so I could see the label on the cover: Private Property. Keep Out!

"I'm sorry, Lily," I said. "But I wanted to tell you that your stories are great. They're really entertaining and totally wacky."

She scowled. "What do you mean?"

"Well, like in 'Dark Days.' All those bad things

that happened to Linda—it's hardly ever that way in real life."

"How do you know?" she asked.

"I just do," I told her. "Like, take us, for example. Sure, lots of bad things have happened to us. We lost Dad, and we are poor. But Mom isn't going to die for a long, long time, and she's working hard to make more money. Besides, we still have each other, and I would never let you go. I'll always be your big sister."

"My nosy big sister," Lily said, looking a little less mad.

"As if you've never snooped in my stuff," I countered.

She started to protest, but I pounced on her, pinning her to the bed in a big bear hug. "You're bossy," Lily complained.

"You're a pest," I replied, and pressed my cheek against hers.

When Lily revealed that she'd been sticking the piles of clean laundry into her closet, I chewed her out for spending all her time in outer space and then helped her fold it all. After putting on a clean pair of jeans and my favorite turtleneck, I headed downstairs and flipped through the newspaper, looking for the movie schedule. I was about to call Mita to suggest going to the two-dollar matinee in Kent when I caught sight of Daisy out the window.

She was in the backyard. Having raked and bagged all the leaves—and there'd been tons—she was now cutting the scraggly brown grass with an old push mower. She was never able to get the gas-powered mower to work again.

Guilt crept into my heart. I really wanted to see the new Tom Cruise movie, but . . .

"Mom, can I borrow the car for a quick errand?" I called out.

"Sure," she answered.

Instead of calling Mita, I made a trip to Appleby's Hardware. Cath's dad helped me pick out the parts I needed. Back home, I put on a jacket and a pair of old gloves and went out to the garage.

When Daisy came up, I was taking the lawn mower apart. "You don't know how to do that," she said.

"Give me a little credit, okay?" I mopped my forehead on the sleeve of my jacket. "Mr. Appleby says if I unscrew this"—I tossed aside a greasy bolt—"and put in a new one of these . . ."

Fifteen minutes later we put some gas in the mower and Daisy gave the cord a pull. It started right up. "You did it!" she exclaimed.

"How about that?" I said with satisfaction. "I'm a regular Ms. Fix-it."

"So we've got the lawn mower working." She gave me an ironic grin. Her hair's growing out—it looked pretty cute, although I knew better than to say so. "Just in time for the first snow."

"Better late than never," I pointed out.

*   *   *

I helped Daisy finish up the yard work, then collapsed at the table in the breakfast nook with a bag of potato chips. All that work had given me a gigantic appetite. As I was gobbling them down Laurel stopped in to grab a can of generic cola from the fridge. I noticed she was wearing a jacket and scarf. "Going over to Jack's?" I guessed.

"Yep."

"How come you guys don't play at our house?"

Laurel shrugged. "It's quieter over there. He doesn't have any brothers or sisters."

"I kind of like sisters, myself," I said.

"Well, Mr. and Mrs. Harrison *want* me to come over," Laurel said. "They plan special stuff for us to do. Last weekend Mr. Harrison taught me how to play backgammon. Today we're going horseback riding."

Suddenly I had a feeling I knew what was going on with Laurel—why she was running over to Jack's all the time. And I figured something else out, too. This is turning into the day I pay back all the favors these guys did for me after I broke up with Parker, I thought. My sisters have been needing me, I realized, as much as I needed them.

I offered Laurel the chips, and she took one. "It's weird sometimes, just having one parent, isn't it?" I asked after a moment.

Laurel shrugged again.

"I miss talking to Dad about stuff," I continued. "And Mom's so busy now, with work and all, sometimes she's not around when I need her, either."

"It's just not fair," Laurel burst out. "We used to be a perfect family, and now everything's awful."

"So Jack's family is perfect?"

She nodded. "He has both his parents. He gets all their attention. And they can afford to buy him whatever he wants and take him all these fun places."

"He's an only child, though. Don't you think that gets lonely sometimes?"

"Maybe," she admitted, "but I'd still trade with him in a minute."

I crunched one last chip, then wiped my hands on a napkin. "Sometimes I wish I could go back in time to when Dad was alive," I told Laurel. "Stop the clock right there."

Laurel gazed at me, her eyes suddenly bright with tears. "But we can't, can we?"

I shook my head. "No. We have to be there for each other in new ways." I put my arms around Laurel, praying that Henry wasn't in one of her coat pockets. "And if we do that, we'll be okay. We'll make it."

Thanksgiving came and went and then, suddenly, it was December. By now I figured that Stephen had probably forgotten about me, but I still found myself thinking about him at odd moments, like this Saturday morning as I sat at the kitchen table eating oatmeal and watching the snow falling outside the window. What's he doing right now? I wondered.

Lily breezed into the kitchen, wearing an *I Dream of Jeannie*–style harem costume. "You're eating breakfast?" she asked. "It's lunchtime!"

Yawning, I glanced at the clock. Lily was right—it was almost noon. "I went to a party at Cath's last night," I told her.

She hopped onto a chair next to me. "Well, hurry up. We're going to cut down a Christmas tree!"

"We are?"

She nodded. "Mom said so. Everyone's going, even Laurel. You need to get dressed!"

I spooned up the last bite of oatmeal. "Is that what you're wearing?"

Lily glanced down at her clothes. "I'll put a snowsuit on over it, of course," she said, rolling her eyes.

Fifteen minutes later, decked out in boots, hats, mittens, and parkas, we marched across the snowy lawn, heading for the woods behind our house. Daisy carried a handsaw, Laurel had some rope looped over her shoulder, and Mom pulled the old Flexible Flyer sled.

"Here's one," Lily said, pointing to the first pine we came across.

"Way too small," Daisy judged. "The best trees are farther in."

As we walked on into the woods I remembered past Decembers. Cutting down the Christmas tree was always Dad's project. "I didn't think we were going to do it this year," I confessed to Mom as we took turns hopping over a half-frozen brook. "I thought maybe we'd just buy a tree."

"But it's such a special ritual," she replied. "It's always meant so much to you girls."

"You're right," I agreed. "It wouldn't really seem like Christmas without a tree from our own woods."

We moved on, our footsteps muffled by the snow. Lily and Laurel skipped ahead, Laurel hunting for deer and fox tracks, Lily's green-and-red stocking cap bouncing. Daisy stopped. "How about that tree?" she called, waving a mittened hand.

We circled the evergreen. It was about six feet tall, and its branches were nice and full except for one flat side. "It's a little bald over here," I pointed out.

"We'll turn that side to the wall," Mom said. "No tree is perfect."

"True." I grinned at Daisy. "Okay. Let's start sawing!"

She and I took turns, and in five minutes the tree fell to the snowy ground with a thump. We hauled it onto the sled, securing its trunk with the rope. Then we all grabbed hold of the rope and pulled the sled toward home.

"Let's sing a Christmas carol," Daisy suggested.

"How about 'Hark, the Herald Angels Sing'?" said Mom.

We shouted out the carol, our breath frosty in the cold air. Back at the house, outside the door, we stood the tree up and shook the snow from its branches. "It's a good tree," Mom declared with satisfaction.

Her cheeks were red from the cold, and her eyes were sparkling, and she had snowflakes in her hair—she looked beautiful. I felt a sudden surge of love for her and for my sisters. It had been a tough year, full of change and loss, but somehow we'd made it through. And I loved my mother and sisters more than I ever had before. I remembered last spring and summer, how I'd tried to be someone different to please Parker, how ashamed and resentful I'd been of my family's poverty. Now I knew what really mattered, and this was it.

"It's a great tree," I said, smiling at my mother.

Fourteen

"Deck the halls with boughs of holly, fa la la la la, la la la la," Lily belted out at the top of her lungs.

It was a wintry Sunday afternoon before Christmas, and we were doing just what the carol said, decking the halls. Laurel was winding pine boughs around the banister. Lily stood on a step stool to arrange holly sprigs on top of the mantel while Daisy wove a wreath for the front door. My project was to make a table centerpiece out of fruit and nuts.

"The house looks festive," Mom said, joining us in the living room. "You girls did a nice job."

"We're going to have an awesome Christmas," Daisy predicted cheerfully.

We'd already agreed that this year, to save money, we'd exchange homemade gifts. The holiday meal would be simple. Of course, with Dad gone, everything about Christmas would feel different. But Daisy's right, I thought. We can still be happy.

Her arms folded tightly across her chest, Mom gazed distractedly at Daisy's half-finished Christmas wreath. "Actually, girls, while you're all together," she said, her tone suddenly more serious, "I suppose this is as good a time as any."

"For what?" Laurel asked.

"I have some news," she began, perching on the arm of a chair.

"Good or bad?" Daisy asked.

"A little of both," Mom replied. "First of all, I'm going to be really busy between now and Christmas. I'm catering three parties."

"Mom, that's terrific!" I exclaimed. "You're almost ready to start your own company."

"Well, I'm not going to quit my job yet, but I am thinking along those lines," she admitted.

Laurel reached up and gave her a hug. I beamed at Mom, so proud of her I was ready to burst. "Yippee!" cheered Lily.

"So, that's the good news," Mom went on. "Thanks to the extra income from the catering, we don't qualify for public aid anymore. But it's still going to be a struggle to make ends meet." I saw Mom's arm tighten around Laurel's shoulders; she gazed at each of us in turn. "I've given it lots of thought, and it looks as if there's only one sure way to take the financial pressure off." She paused to take a deep breath. "We're going to have to sell the house."

A shocked silence fell over us. We all stared at Mom with stunned expressions. Lily's mouth dropped open. Laurel blinked. "Sell the house?" Daisy repeated in disbelief.

"I wish there was an alternative, I really do," Mom said. "But the property taxes are just too high."

"But where will we live?" Lily wailed. "Are we going to be homeless?"

"Oh, honey, of course not." Mom hurried over to Lily and scooped her up in a reassuring hug. "We'll rent a smaller place. I've already found a cute three-bedroom apartment right in town."

"Does it have a yard?" asked Laurel.

"I'm afraid not," Mom said.

Laurel's face fell. Her hutches were full of animals again, and I knew she was worrying about where they would all live. "But what about the rabbit and the baby squirrel and—"

"We'll have to find other homes for them," Mom told Laurel. "I'll go over to the Wildlife Rescue Center with you and see if they can help."

"Do I have to get rid of Henry, too?" Laurel's voice was small.

"We can't have any pets at all," Mom said. "I'm sorry, sweetheart."

I'd always detested Laurel's furry friends, but now I couldn't help feeling sorry for her. Then something else occurred to me. "The apartment has only three bedrooms?" I asked Mom. "You mean, we'll have to share?"

Mom looked at me over Lily's head, her eyes pleading for support. "I know you're used to privacy, but if we save money on rent, we'll have more left for extras."

Immediately I felt bad that I'd sounded selfish. I'd grown up a lot since my sixteenth birthday, when I'd pouted about having to give up camp in order to get a summer job. We were a family, and we had to stick together through thick and thin. I was Mom's oldest daughter—I should back her up, not criticize her.

"An apartment sounds cozy," I said with as much false cheer as I could muster. "It might even be fun sharing a room." I turned to Daisy. "Like a slumber party, right?"

Daisy nodded, but her eyes were swimming with tears. "Yeah," she said, and her voice was strained and reedy. "It'll be great."

Laurel sniffled loudly. Lily buried her face in Mom's neck and began to sob. Daisy was still struggling to hold back tears, and so was I. Reaching out, I took Daisy's hand and gave it a firm squeeze. "We'll be together," I said. "That's what matters most."

"Isn't there anything we can do?" Daisy begged. "I'll get a job."

"And I promise to help out more around the house . . . ," Lily added.

Mom held my gaze as she hugged Lily tight. "I know we'll all be sad to leave this house, but Rose is right."

Lily nodded, her face smudged with tears. Laurel hugged herself, her feet tucked up and her arms wrapped around her knees. Daisy and I continued to hold hands, giving each other strength. We sat quietly like that for a long time, each lost in her own thoughts about what it would mean to say good-bye to the only home we'd ever known.

Christmas wasn't like any other we'd celebrated before. We were all missing Dad even more than usual. And there weren't very many packages under the tree. But that's okay, I told myself, trying not to feel sad about it. There are more important things than gifts.

"When can we open our presents?" Lily asked, hopping up and down impatiently.

Mom curled up on the living room sofa, a mug of hot coffee in her hand. "I'm ready," she said. "Why don't you start?"

Daisy took over Dad's job of handing out the presents. She found a box with Lily's name on it. "Here's one," she said.

Lily read the tag. "It's from Rose," she said. It took her about a millisecond to tear the paper off. "A new notebook, and Rose decorated it!"

"If you're going to be a famous writer, you might as well have the right materials," I told her.

"Here's one for you, Laurel," Daisy said. "From Lily."

"It's an envelope," Laurel said, tilting her head. "What is it?"

"Look inside and see!" Lily urged.

Laurel opened the envelope and pulled out a single sheet of paper decorated with animal stickers. Her eyes began to sparkle. "Lily wrote a poem for me."

"Read it out loud," I said.

"'Nearest in age, we fight the most, too,'" Laurel read. "'Sometimes I wish there wasn't any you. But deep inside, I know you really care. I'd be sad if you weren't always there.'"

"Do you like it?" Lily asked anxiously.

Laurel nodded. "It's a great present. Thanks, Lily."

"I wrote a poem for everybody," Lily said, blushing with pride.

"That was a wonderful idea," Mom said.

We continued opening our gifts. Mom had sewn a dozen hair scrunchies out of pretty scraps of fabric—three for each of us, including Daisy, whose hair was long enough to tie back again. "Look!" Daisy said, holding up a shoe box Laurel had covered in a collage of sports pictures. "This will be perfect for storing my baseball cards. Thanks!"

There was one more present for Laurel. I handed her a bulky, heavy package. "Wow. What is it?" she asked.

"Open it and see," I told her.

Laurel ripped off the paper. Inside was a brand-new hamster-size cage with a sliding tray at the bottom. I'd gotten an extra-special deal on it at Appleby's Hardware. "What's this for?" Laurel wondered.

"It's for Henry," I explained. "I talked Mom into asking the landlord if you could keep one of your animals, and it's okay as long as Henry stays in his cage."

"Oh, Rose." Laurel's smile was brighter than the lights on the Christmas tree. "Thank you so, so much!"

There was only one gift left under the tree. "It's for Rose," Daisy announced.

I took the small, flat box. "Feels like a CD," I said. "But who . . ." Then I read the tag. "From Stephen? How did this get here?"

"He left it on the porch," Mom said. "Actually, I invited him in for a cup of cocoa. He's very nice."

"Yes," I agreed softly. "He is." Stephen was here? I thought. Drinking cocoa with my mother— and I didn't even know it?

I looked at the tag: *To Rose*, it read. *We aren't as different as you think. Yours always, Stephen*. My mother didn't say anything else, and neither did I. I opened the present. I can't say that I was surprised to find it was a Sheryl Crowe CD. "I can't believe he did that," I said, swallowing tears.

"He must still like you," Lily said.

"Do you still like him?" asked Laurel.

I nodded. "Yeah. Isn't that dumb?"

"I don't think it's dumb," Daisy said. "I mean, I'm not ever going to have a boyfriend, but I think Stephen is great."

I put the CD with my other presents. He was great, but I'd blown it. And my pride was still in the way—I couldn't go after him now, and he probably wouldn't take me back even if I did. "It doesn't matter. It's ancient history," I said, drying my eyes.

We all looked at the Christmas tree. There

were no more packages. Lily's lower lip pushed out in a pout. "It used to take *forever* for us to open all our presents," she recalled sadly.

"I know what we can do," Mom said. "Let's all give one more gift to the person sitting to our left."

"How?" asked Laurel. "There aren't any more presents."

"A gift of service or of time or talent," Mom explained. "There are lots of nice things we can do for each other. You start, Rose."

"Well, I'm sitting next to you, Mom," I said, smiling at her. "You work so hard, I should think of a way to make your life easier. How about . . . taking over one of your chores? I'll take out the garbage every week."

"That would be tremendous," Mom said. "Thanks, honey."

"My turn!" Lily said. "I have Rose. From now on, I'll bring you your laundry on time *and* I'll sort it and put it away for you."

"Good deal," I said. "Thanks, Lil."

Mom was gazing at Daisy, her cheek propped thoughtfully on her fingertips. "I have Daisy. Hmmm," she murmured. "How do I help my best helper?"

"Cook her something, Mom," Lily suggested.

"That's a good idea. I'll bake a care package for Daisy's whole team every time there's an away game."

"That would be great, Mom," said Daisy. "We're always starving on the bus ride home.

Okay, I have Laurel. I know. When we get to the new apartment, since the only real pet you can have is Henry, I'll help you set up a fish tank."

Laurel's eyes brightened. "You're the best, Daze." She was the last to go. "I have Lily," she said, eyeing her younger sister. "We're going to share a room in the new place, which means we might fight more than ever. So my present to you is that I promise I won't pick any fights with you even if you do something that really, really annoys me. And if we do start arguing, I'll say that you were right and stop. For a month," she added.

"And maybe a month will be all it takes for you two to get along better," said Mom.

"That was fun," Lily said. "Now I feel like I got everything I wanted for Christmas."

Judging from everybody's faces, we all felt that way. I gave Lily a hug. "Me too."

"Three large boxes, totally full," Daisy declared, huffing and puffing. "And that was just the coat closet!"

It was January 1, and we were ringing in the New Year by packing boxes. "It's amazing how much stuff we've accumulated over the years, isn't it?" Mom agreed as she rolled up the hall carpet.

Laurel thundered down the stairs. "I've finished packing my room," she reported. "Now what should I do?"

"You and Daisy could tackle the garage," Mom

suggested. "But don't strain yourselves. Leave the heavy stuff for Stan and Mr. Smith."

Our neighbor and his son were going to help us move our furniture and boxes over to the new apartment tomorrow. One more day, I thought as I placed volumes of the *Encyclopædia Britannica* in a box, and then we'll all walk out of this house for the very last time.

When the box was full, I taped it shut and labeled it. Then I threw on a parka and headed out to the garage to see if Daisy and Laurel needed help.

I found Laurel standing by her empty animal hutches. "Are you okay?" I asked.

I'd assumed she was crying, but instead she turned to me with a smile. "I'll really miss the yard and the barn and our trees," she said, "and the crocuses in the spring and the fox we sometimes see at the edge of the woods and the robin's nest and our view of the ocean."

"I will, too," I agreed, wondering why she didn't seem sadder about it.

"I'll be glad to have a fish tank, though," she added. "And Henry, of course."

I smiled at her and headed toward the garage. Daisy was inside, a half-packed cardboard box in front of her. She was standing very still, lost in thought. "What's that?" I asked her.

She held up the baseball mitt she was holding. "Dad's old mitt, from when he was in high school. The one he used to wear when we played catch, back when he taught me how to throw."

I smiled sadly, but Daisy didn't seem that upset. "It's all Dad's stuff in here," she observed as she dropped the mitt in the box. "Fishing gear, tools, car parts."

"We probably don't need most of it," I remarked.

"Probably not, but I'm packing it, anyway," she said cheerfully. "Well . . . maybe not the car parts."

I decided to finish packing my own stuff. Back inside the house, I walked down the hall to the staircase. Just as I passed the storage cupboard under the stairs, its door popped open and Lily crawled out. "What on earth were you doing in there?" I asked, raising my eyebrows.

Lily brushed the dust from her hands. "I'm saying good-bye to all my old secret hiding places," she explained matter-of-factly. "I'm sure the new apartment will have some good ones, but it might take me a while to sniff them out."

"There's bound to be a closet or two," I replied.

Lily trotted off toward the kitchen, probably to say good-bye to the pantry. Upstairs, I paused in the hall near my bedroom door. Bending forward, I squinted at some faint pencil marks on the wall. I smiled, remembering the last time Dad had lined us up to see how tall we were. It was years ago, but I could almost see the ghosts of the little girls we were.

My bedroom was a mess of half-packed suitcases and boxes. Paperback books spilled out of a plastic milk crate, and another crate was stuffed with shoes.

Instead of resuming the task of emptying dresser drawers, though, I went over to the window and leaned my arms on the sill. I followed Lighthouse Road with my eyes, tracing it to its end, where the pines and rocks tumbled into the sea. This had been my window, my view, through all the seasons, year in and year out, ever since I was a little girl.

And I'm sad to be leaving, I thought, blinking back a tear. How come no one else is?

It was dusk when the doorbell rang. When I opened the door, I saw Cath, Mita, and Rox standing on the porch. "Hi," I said, surprised. "Are you guys here to help me pack?"

"No, we're here to get you to go out with us tonight," said Rox.

"You need a break from all this work," Cath agreed.

"We were thinking about the Rusty Nail," Mita put in. "What do you say?"

"Thanks, you guys," I said, and gave a sentimental sniffle, "but it's our last night in the old house, you know? I think my sisters and Mom and I will want to just be together and—"

"Speak for yourself," Laurel said, coming up behind me. "I'm going over to Jack's tonight."

"I'm going to the movies with some friends," said Daisy, appearing in the hall.

"Vera Schenkel invited us to come by for supper," Mom announced, emerging from the family room. "I'll take Lily. Why don't you go out with your friends, Rose?"

"Well," I mumbled. If I didn't go to the Rusty Nail, it looked like I'd be sitting home alone. Thanks a lot! I thought, feeling left out. "I guess I'll go with you. Since no one else wants to hang out with me," I added, whining a little.

"Great," said Daisy.

"Here's your coat," Laurel said, tossing it to me.

"Have a good time!" Mom called.

The four of us squeezed into the cab of Mr. Appleby's pickup truck. Cath drove, Mita sat in the middle, and I sat on Rox's lap. "So, am I a sappy fool?" I asked my friends. "How come nobody else in my family seems bummed about moving? It's like they know something they're not telling me."

Cath and Mita exchanged a meaningful glance. "Maybe they've just decided that moving's not so bad," Cath suggested.

"Maybe," I said, unconvinced.

I was still feeling a little put out when we parked at the Rusty Nail, but as soon as I got inside I was glad I'd gone out. As usual, the music was great. Cath's and Rox's boyfriends, Tony and Kurt, were there, and we took turns dancing with them. We played a game of pool—Kurt and I beat Mita and Rox—then danced some more. I was having a good time when suddenly I spotted a familiar-looking blond woman across the room.

"Whoa, Mita!" I said, grabbing her arm and making her spill her soda. "I think that's my mom. It *is* my mom! What's she doing here?"

Before I could charge over and ask Mom why on earth she was hanging out at the Rusty Nail on a Saturday night when she was supposed to be having dinner at the Schenkels', Bruno, the deejay, stopped the dance music. "It's open mike night, folks," he announced, "and for starters tonight, we have something a little different. Our first performer is here all the way from Seagate Academy. He's singing this song for someone in the audience, and I think she knows who she is. Everybody give a big hand to—"

"Stephen!" I gasped.

My eyes bulged in surprise, and I stared at Cath. She grinned and gave me a shrug. Stephen hopped onstage and took the microphone from Bruno, then beckoned to someone down in the crowd. To my amazement, three other people joined him onstage: Daisy, Laurel, and Lily!

"'If I fell in love with you, would you promise to be true and help me understand,'" Stephen began singing. It was "If I Fell."

As Stephen sang my favorite Beatles song, with my sisters providing the background vocals, I started to cry. They were terrible—Stephen's voice kept cracking on the high notes, and my sisters are all tone-deaf—but everyone was clapping wildly, anyway. "I can't believe this," I said to Cath, Mita, and Rox, sniffling. "This is absolutely the craziest, sweetest thing anyone's ever done for me."

As he sang, Stephen stared straight down into my eyes. "'Cause I couldn't stand the pain. And I would be sad if our new love was in vain . . .'" My heart brimmed with happiness because I knew what he was trying to tell me. In this crazy way he was showing me that he *could* fit into my world, and I could fit into his, if we both were willing to make the effort. That's what love is all about.

When the song ended, Stephen and my sisters got the loudest round of applause I've ever heard at the Rusty Nail. My friends cheered wildly, and so did my mom, and so did I. Stephen jumped down from the stage and made his way toward me. "Rose," he said, taking both my hands in his. "I know a song can't say everything, but do you think we could—"

"Oh, shut up and kiss me, Stephen Mathias," I said, pulling him to me. And as everyone cheered even louder, that's exactly what he did.

Fifteen

"I was wondering why everyone was in such a good mood, considering we're about to leave our home," I told Stephen later as we sat alone in my living room, surrounded by boxes. "I can't believe you planned that!"

"When I told your family what I had in mind, they were all for it," Stephen said. "I guess they think I'm okay."

"They think you're the greatest," I said, "and so do my friends. They all thought I was nuts to break up with you."

"You were nuts," Stephen said.

We wrapped our arms around each other, and Stephen kissed me. With a happy sigh I rested my head on his shoulder. "I was so stupid and proud," I reflected.

"No, it was my fault," Stephen said, stroking my hair. "I wanted to do something nice for you—the voice lessons—but I didn't think about how it might make you feel."

"I was just so insecure because of what happened with Parker," I told him. "I judged you based on how he treated me. It wasn't fair."

"Do you think we can start over?"

"I'd like that," I said, looking up at him with shining eyes. "But only if you promise you'll shake me if I ever jump to conclusions about someone based on superficial things like how much money they have or what school they go to."

"It's a deal," Stephen said, "if you promise not to make me go skinny-dipping in the Atlantic."

"Okay, if you promise we'll never double-date with Val and Parker."

"Okay, if you promise I don't have to sing at open mike night again."

"Are you kidding? The Rusty Nail wants to sign you up for a regular gig!"

We kissed again, and then I said softly, "Thanks for giving me a second chance, Stephen."

"I knew I'd never meet anyone as special as you ever again." His brown eyes twinkled. "Anyway, you *had* to take me back. Who else would put up with Henry?"

"There should be thunder and lightning and wind and hail," Lily said in a melodramatic tone. The next morning we were watching Stan Smith and his father carry the living room couch—the same one Stephen and I had been kissing on the night before—up the ramp into the rented moving truck. "Or maybe an earthquake or a volcano erupting."

"A volcano in Maine?" I said with a laugh.

It was a beautiful winter day—crisp and sunny.

And it was hard to be too down because moving had turned into a neighborhood block party. Mrs. Smith had brought us a basket of home-baked muffins for breakfast, and the Comiskeys delivered pizzas for lunch. People stopped by to wish us luck and stayed to help carry a box or two. Stephen was there, too, helping Mr. Smith and Stan with the heavy stuff. Somehow Stephen managed to make moving heavy boxes look really cute.

Finally the truck was loaded, and I made plans to see Stephen later, after my sisters and I were somewhat settled in the apartment. My sisters were already in the station wagon, with the windows rolled down so they could say good-bye to their friends. I walked through the house one last time with Mom. "Doesn't look like we missed anything," she said, glancing into the empty hall closet. "I guess it's time to go."

We stepped out the door, and then she turned to lock it with her key. We both knew it was the last time we'd stand on the front porch, the last time we'd walk down the flagstone path to the driveway. We'd already sold the house, and in just a week a new family would be moving in. Mom's eyes were moist, but she held her shoulders square and managed to give me a brave smile. "Don't look back," she advised.

And I didn't.

"Look. We have a view!" Lily and Laurel chorused.

Daisy and I had been debating how to arrange the furniture in our new bedroom. It was going to be cramped, with two twin beds, two dressers, and two desks. Glad to have a distraction, we jogged down the hall to Lily and Laurel's room.

We joined our younger sisters at the window. Sure enough, it looked out over the small town park, beyond which there were storefronts, a church steeple, and a glimpse of the harbor.

"This place isn't half bad," Daisy said.

"I like the way the roof slopes down under the eaves," I said.

"And the smell from Wissinger's Bakery downstairs," Lily said.

Just then the doorbell rang. All four of us raced into the front hall. "I bet it's Stephen," I said.

"Or Jack," Laurel said.

"Maybe it's Kyle," Lily said, poking Daisy in the ribs.

"Shut up, Lily," Daisy said.

Mom answered the door. A man I'd never seen before, thin and tall with glasses and brown, receding hair, stood in the doorway. "Hello," he said, sticking out his hand. He had a nice voice, deep and warm. "I'm Hal Leverett, your new neighbor. Just thought I'd introduce myself and see if you needed any help carting boxes or moving furniture."

"Why, that's nice of you," Mom said, smiling. "Come on in. I was just thinking that I'd like to slide the china cabinet to the other side of the dining room. If it's not too heavy for you . . ."

It wasn't too heavy. After Mr. Leverett had moved the china cabinet, Mom invited him to sit down while she made a pot of tea. Meanwhile Daisy and I unpacked a box of tablecloths and place mats. "Why is he sticking around?" Daisy hissed under her breath.

"Why shouldn't he?" I asked.

"He's flirting with Mom!"

"No, he's not," I said. "He's just being nice."

Her forehead furrowed, Daisy dug into another box labeled Pictures. Locating a framed photo of Dad, she marched across the living room and propped it on the center of the mantel. "Our father," she announced, to no one in particular but loud enough so that Mr. Leverett, sitting in the dining room with Mom, could hear.

I smiled to myself. Suspicious, protective Daisy. As I stored some linens in the buffet, though, I shot a glance at Mom and Mr. Leverett. They did seem to be having a lively conversation. Mr. Leverett made a remark about the bakery downstairs, and Mom laughed. They chatted about their work, and he made her laugh again, drawing comparisons between her catering and his accounting business. "More tea?" she offered.

"Please," he said.

I watched Mom's face as she refilled Mr. Leverett's cup. It's like the clock's been turned back, like she's a year younger, I thought. For a moment I glimpsed the Maggie Walker of old: lighthearted, funny, pretty—all qualities that had been buried under sorrow and worry since Dad died. Mom had been under such a strain for so long; now it was as if winter were ending early. She was ready to bloom, to be herself again.

Suddenly this moving day took on a completely different meaning for me. I realized that for Mom, selling the old house didn't represent failure. The opposite, in fact. It was a triumph—she'd held her family together, and she was going to support us, and she'd done it all on her own. And maybe, as much as we'd all loved the old house, it was better for us to start over someplace fresh. We'd never forget Dad, but here his absence would be less of a presence. We would have a little distance. Perspective.

When I went back to unpacking, I discovered Lily perched on an ottoman in the living room, the notebook I'd given her for Christmas on her knee. "What are you writing?" I asked her.

"A new story," she replied.

"Of course," I said. That's what all of us were doing. One chapter of our lives had ended, but another was beginning.

A week after we moved, Stephen came by to take me out. It was Saturday afternoon and a mild winter day, the kind that smells like thawing earth, like spring. "Your apartment is great," he said as we strolled down the sidewalk, holding hands. "We can walk to just about everything from here."

I knew Stephen was sincere. Besides, I wasn't insecure about this kind of thing anymore. "It's really convenient," I agreed.

"Do you miss your old house?" he asked.

I thought about it. Did I miss it? The big yard, where my sisters and I had chased fireflies on summer nights; the garage, where Dad had repaired his fishing gear and tinkered on various home improvement projects; the swing on the porch, where I'd gotten my first real kiss (from Sully in eighth grade); the bow window in the living room, where we put the Christmas tree so its lights would shine out on the snow in the front yard; the old stove in the kitchen, where Mom baked our birthday cakes.

"I'm glad I'll turn seventeen in the new apartment," I told Stephen, answering his question indirectly. "Because I'm a different person than I was a year ago." I squeezed his hand. "Do you know what I mean?"

He squeezed my hand back. "Yeah, I know what you mean."

We continued to walk along Main Street, past Cecilia's, which was closed for the rest of the winter, and Appleby's Hardware and the Village Market and the Corner Ice Cream Shoppe. The year I turned sixteen had had so many ups and downs, but I knew now that I'd gained more than

I'd lost. It wasn't always easy being an adult, and it wasn't always fun, but I was getting the hang of it. I was growing up. And the year I turned sixteen, I'd fallen in love. Twice. This time, with Stephen, I knew it was for real.

"How does chili at Patsy's sound?" my boyfriend asked me.

"Spicy," I replied. "Last one to the corner buys!"

We raced toward the setting sun together.

@café

Meet the staff of @café:
Natalie, Dylan, Blue, Sam, Tanya, and Jason.
They serve coffee, surf the net,
and share their deepest darkest secrets . . .

#1 Love Bytes
00445-X/$3.99

#2 I'll Have What He's Having
00446-8/$3.99

#3 Make Mine To Go
00447-6/$3.99

#4 Flavor of the Day
00448-4/$3.99

Novels by Elizabeth Craft

Available from Archway Paperbacks
Published by Pocket Books

1430-02

Calling All Sisters

National Sisters' Day is August 2nd!

Celebrate the bonds of sisterhood by telling us about your special relationship with your sister(s) and you could be published and pictured in *Girls' Life* magazine.

In fifty words or less, tell us about your relationship with your sister(s), and send along a photo. Winner gets her essay and photo published in *Girls' Life* magazine!

Send your Sisters' Day/*Girls' Life* essay and photo with your name, age, address, phone number, and parent's (or legal guardian's) signature saying it is okay to publish your entry and photo in *Girls' Life* to:

POCKET BOOKS: SISTERS' DAY/*GIRLS' LIFE* SWEEPSTAKES, 13TH FLOOR 1230 AVENUE OF THE AMERICAS, NEW YORK, NY 10020

Name _____ Age _____

Address_____

City _____State _____Zip Code _____

Phone Number (_____) _____

Parent's Signature _____ 1494 (1of2)

Sisters' Day/*Girls' Life* Sweepstakes Official Rules

1. No purchase necessary. Enter by submitting your entry form and a typed or hand-printed essay that is no longer than 50 words and a photo of you and your sister(s). Please send them with your name, age, address, phone number, and parent's (or legal guardian's) signature saying it is okay to publish your entry and photo in *Girls' Life* to Pocket Books: Sisters' Day/Girls' Life Sweepstakes, 13th Floor, 1230 Avenue of the Americas, New York, NY 10020. Signed submissions constitute permission to publish entries in Girls' Life. Entries must be received by December 31, 1998. Not responsible for lost, late, damaged, stolen, illegible, mutilated, incomplete, postage-due, not delivered entries or for typographical errors in the entry form or rules. Entries are void if they are in whole or in part illegible, incomplete or damaged. You may enter as often as you wish, but each entry must be mailed separately. Winner will be selected at random from all eligible entries received in a drawing to be held on or about 1/7/99. Winner will be notified by mail.

2. Prize: essay and photo published in Girls' Life magazine (*approx. retail value: $500.00*). Prize not transferable and may not be substituted except by sponsor.

3. The sweepstakes is open to sisters ages 10-17 (as of June 9, 1998) who reside in the United States or Canada (excluding Quebec). Void in Puerto Rico and wherever prohibited or restricted by law. All federal, state and local laws apply. Employees and their families living in the same household, of Girls' Life and Viacom Inc., and their respective subsidiaries, affiliates, agencies, and participating retailers are not eligible.

4. The odds of winning depend upon the number of eligible entries received.

5. If a winner is a Canadian resident, then she must correctly answer a skill-based question administered by mail.

6. All expenses on receipt and use of prize including federal, state and local taxes are the sole responsibility of the winner. Winner's parent or legal guardian must execute and return an Affidavit of Eligibility and Liability/Publicity release within 15 days of notification attempt or an alternate winner will be selected.

7. Winner or winner's parents (or legal guardians) on winner's behalf grants to Pocket Books and Girls' Life the right to use her name and entry for any advertising, promotion, and publicity purposes without further compensation to or permission from the winner, except where prohibited by law, and the right to adapt, edit, and publish the winning entry.

8. By participating in this sweepstakes, entrants agree to be bound by these rules and the decision of the judges and sweepstakes sponsors, which are final in all matters relating to the sweepstakes.

9. The sweepstakes sponsors shall have no liability for any injury, loss or damage of any kind arising out of participation in this sweepstakes or the acceptance or use of the prize.

10. For the name of the prize winner (available after 1/15/99), send a stamped, self-addressed envelope to Prize Winner, Pocket Books: Sisters' Day/Girls' Life Sweepstakes, 13th Floor, 1230 Avenue of the Americas, New York, NY 10020.